THE DEVIL'S RELICS

An Emer Harte Mystery

Martin Malone

www.owlfellaspress.ie

Owl Fella's Press acknowledges The Arts Council of Ireland
for its financial support.

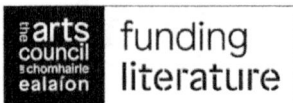

ALSO BY MARTIN MALONE

Novels
Us
After Kafra
The Broken Cedar
The Silence of the Glasshouse
The Only Glow of the Day
Valley of the Peacock Angel
Black Rose Days
Iapetus, '81

Short Stories
The Mango War & other stories
Deadly Confederacies & other stories
This Cruel Station, stories
In the White Country, novella & stories

Radio Plays
The Devil's Garden
Song of the Small Bird
Rosanna Nightwalker
Stage
Rosanna Nightwalker, the wrens of the Curragh

eBooks
The Winter, is it Past? The Curragh Executions
Isaiah's Reach, novella
The Connaught Rangers, Indian Mutiny, 1920 (Newbridge Connection)
Rosanna Nightwalker, the play
*

Screen Options
After Kafra (also development)
The Broken Cedar

Martin Murt Malone

...was commissioned for Lines of Vision, Irish Writers on Art, The National Art Gallery and also by BBC Radio 4, BBC World Service, RTE Radio 1. And published by Doire Press, Owl Fella's Press, Simon & Schuster UK, Phoenix UK, Thames & Hudson UK, O'Brien Press, Brandon Press, Stand UK, The Stinging Fly, The Dublin Review, The Sunday Tribune, The Irish Times, The Sunday Times, The Sunday Independent, The Malahat Review (Can), The Fiddlehead (Can), The Cortland Review (USA), Passages, FISH Publishing, New Island, Poolbeg Press and Maverick House.

PRAISE FOR MALONE'S WORK:

As strong a collection as you are likely to read all year
Patrick McCabe *(Breakfast on Pluto).*

But the one that sticks in the mind is Martin Malone's *elegiac*
account of taking his ailing Dad, a former jockey, to see Jack Yeats's
Before the Start (1915)
Claire Wrathall, Arts Quarterly UK.

Powerfully moving story that will touch the senses
June Edwards, The Sunday Tribune.

'...if you have not already come across Martin Malone, catch up
now...'
Books Ireland, Paula O'Hare.

'...there will be few better books published this year.'
Eilish O'Hanlon, The Irish Independent.

Awards: a selection

The Sunday Independent/John B Keane Literary Prize

RTE Francis MacManus Short Story Award

The Inaugural Cecil D Lewis Literary Award

The Dennis O'Driscoll Literary Prize

The Killarney Bookshop 250 International Short Story Award

Ireland's Own Open Short Story Competition

Fallen Leaves Short Story Competition

Literature Bursaries, Arts Council of Ireland.

Translations: Short stories – Danish colleges, Italian. San Jose State
University, California U.S.A.

Dedication

For my wife, Valerie.

CONTENTS

FOREWORD

Most of a writer's output is rooted during their developing years, it's said. But I'm unsure if that's the case – my field experience with UNIFIL on five occasions, commencing from age 28, ranging from 1985 to 1998, yielded several novels, a memoir, and a short story collection. Two of the novels were optioned for screen. *After Kafra* concerned a military policeman bringing Lebanon home with him in the form of PTSD, and how he and others handled this, or didn't. *The Broken Cedar* followed an MP sergeant returning to Lebanon to search for and retrieve his father's remains, also a soldier, kidnapped almost 20 years before. *The Lebanon Diaries* is a gutted memoir for fears of libel, which remains libellous even if the words are true, while *In the White Country, a novella and stories* deals with the repercussions of low-level espionage in a south Lebanese hilltop hamlet overlooking UNIFIL Headquarters. These stories are mostly revised publications and radio broadcasts... There's a new work, a fictional one, eight years in the writing... which I'll introduce after the next paragraphs.

Paul Brady's beautiful ballad refers to Lebanon's burning skies. They've been burning since the mid-70s, when internecine feuds among Christian, Muslim, and Palestinian refugees resulted in a viciously fought civil war. Until then, since achieving independence from France in 1943, Lebanon was prosperous. The country's first general elections held in over 20 years in 1992 saw Amal ousted and Hezbollah enter government... Over the following years, Israel withdrew to the internationally recognised border (the Shabaa Farms are disputed) with its neighbour. Aside from its economy in tatters, and the Beirut port disaster causing the loss of many lives, Lebanon experienced comparative peace... intermittently, that is. There is, however, nothing as wanton as the latest incursions by the Israeli army and Air Force into Lebanon and the Palestinian lands, ignited by

1

the massacre of unsuspecting and unarmed Israeli citizens on Oct 7th.

I sometimes wonder about the children and people whom I knew on both sides of the conflict, caught up in all of this madness and mayhem; adults now with their own children, and in old age, and with every hope in front of them torched by violence, with every combatant's conscience stained, if not now, at some point down the road, if a soul is to ripen, become mature. Memory can have a hard bite on the heart. Hatred breeds nothing, only recurring cycles of violence... and that's what makes it so impossible to comprehend – to see hatred wrapped as a body bag covering a dead child, knowing it's a seed sown to a world no reasonable person would wish for. The skies mimic Dante's Inferno, the land is charred, and there's the corrosion of human kindness – but perhaps – when I think on it – if a war were fought in Heaven... it probably shouldn't come as a surprise that humankind would follow suit.

*

The Devil's Relics, an Emer Harte novel, published by Owl Fella's Press...

Emer Harte's choice of career is unconsciously introduced at an early age when she discovers the remains of her best friend's mother, missing for several months. After a spell with the Irish civic police, she switches career to the Irish army, and is a military police officer serving in south Lebanon when she's detailed to investigate the reported disappearances of two Irish UN peacekeepers on leave with their units touring party in Israel... The clues run as a lighted fuse toward chaos.

*

A rose of a day, summer sun on its petals. Islands of furze in full Midas bloom surrounded the children. Emer peaked her hand to her eyes to shield from the sun's midday glare.

She counted to eighteen and turned about. 'Ready or not, here I come!'

Pause.

'NINETEEN! ...TWENTY!'

The sun had scorched the grass, hardened the impressions of horse hoofs that stretched to the all-weather gallop just past a cairn of wood chippings.

She was about to set off, eyes aimed at a trail leading between gorse, when she heard Hannah scream. Emer's heart sparked a small jump.

Her sister screamed again. Short, sharp, and terrifying.

Cupping her hands about her mouth, she shouted, 'Hannah!'

She couldn't have gone too far into the furze. Emer had only counted to twenty. A touch to her elbow. Her knees buckled and her breath froze.

'What's wrong with Hannah?' G.I.'s voice quivered.

She clamped her lips, not wanting G.I. to know how badly he'd scared her. A frantic rustling noise in the furze. Sobbing, drawing her breath, her green eyes wide, Hannah emerged from the depth of furze in which she'd been hiding. Terror stricken.

'What's the matter?' Emer approached her.

Hannah pointed behind her, unable to speak.

'Maybe we should go,' G.I. suggests, standing on Emer's shadow.

Hannah shivered; her teeth chattered. She put her hands to her upper arms, digging her nails into the flesh.

G.I.'s voice was weak. 'Emer, come on. Vibes. I have bad vibes about this place.'

'You get bad vibes about most places.'

'I do not.'

'Yes, you do.'

'Hannah?' Emer said, stepping in front of G.I., effectively telling him to shut it.

Hannah's eyeballs bulged as though the words in her mouth had detoured to their sockets. Spines of furze were caught up in her hair. Suddenly she broke into a run in the direction of home. Watching her sister, Emer thought to follow her but stayed put and suppressed an urge to call her name.

'Don't you think we should go after her, eh?' G.I. said.

'No!' Then quietly, 'No.'

'What then? She's your sister. If she were mine... I would. I would do that.'

'I'm going to see what scared Hannah – that's what. You should want to find that out, too. Right?'

'Ah, shit. Aw, come on, let's go home, Emer, please. I've got a bad feeling about this.'

Even back then, she'd pushed things, went too far... Here... now... in south Lebanon, she had done the same... For every push forward there's a push back... in some form.

She'd owned a bad feeling too. But Mam and Dad were at home and would ask two questions: why had she let Hannah run home in such a state, and why hadn't she looked to see what had frightened her sister half to death?

Hannah was a figure in the distance, passing a woman walking her Dalmatians and a couple of kids kicking an orange ball in the air, near to a broken-up goalpost, its sole upright post giving the finger to the world.

For moments Emer gazed at the Wicklow mountains; mountains backdropped by blue skies, their flanks purple heathered. Cloud shadow then drifted across the ridges and she thought the mountains' spines must feel as cold as her own.

'Be a hero,' she said, more to herself, mustering a streak of determination.

G.I. muttered, 'Heroes get killed, don't you know?'

'Are you going to let me go in by myself?'

G.I.'s cheeks shaded apple red. Though he resembled his father, he had none of that man's bitterness or the habit of narrowing his eyes when he looked at people.

Edging towards the furze, Emer dropped to her hunkers. G.I. behind, panting. 'Wait... Wait.'

Glancing over her shoulder she saw him struggling to loosen a blade from the housing of his Swiss army knife. Dropping the knife, he picked it up only to drop it again. Snatching it, she freed the blade and then returned the knife. His fingernails were bitten to the quick, she'd noticed. His fingers stubby, dirt-ingrained, and Emer imagined his eyes held the fear of Coliseum-bound Christians.

It was cool under the furze and darkish. The air smelt a little of pine, of furze coconut and vanilla. Beads of sheep dirt scattered here and there, fox litter. Goat, too. Missing was the ammoniac reek of horse dung for it to be a proper shit party. G.I. farted. Long winded. A melody of nerves.

Emer reflected from her Lebanese-based billet, that another odour was present – but she hadn't copped on to it at first. Perhaps poor G.I. had camouflaged it...

'They're not smelly,' he said. 'My farts usually smell like magnesium, y'know.'

'You stink.'

'What do you mean? I had a bath last night, after watching *The A-Team*. I even used the last of Mammy's special bath stuff. She's not around to use it anymore, and she used to say, "Waste not, want not." That's from the Bible, it is.'

'Quieten, would you?'

Inching forward, G.I. muttering and moaning about his new tracksuit being dirtied and how Aunt Tam will bite the arse off him and have him in the charity shop first thing tomorrow morning trying on new cast-offs.

'...she's the crabbiest aul bitch, Emer. Only does the toast on one side. Scroogie mean. I asked her for that book you wanted to read, about your man lost on a desert island with a black fella.' Pauses for breath. 'What was his name, the black lad?'

'Friday. Man Friday.'

'I knew it was something like that – anyway, she ignored me, but at least I asked her for you, Emer.'

'I ordered it from the library.'

'Mean scroogie, she is.'

She considered asking if his aunt still hit him but knew he wouldn't say. His father did. He also belted anyone he thought would be too afraid to hit him back.

Ahead she saw the bramble bones of the gorse; dry, thick, gnarled branches. Ignoring the razoring of needles at her face and body she sank lower and wormed her way through a place where the bramble had knitted into a tight pattern. Emerging in a small clearing, she smiled. The sun shone and the sky was a vivid blue. The contrails of a jet were fading to nothingness.

G.I. hauled himself up and brushed himself down. Revealed his exertions in a loud struggle for a steady breath.

'What's... what's so funny?' he asked of her smile.

Pointing, she said, 'I'd say that's what terrified Hannah. She's as squeamish...'

G.I. sighed and nodded as though one action had triggered the other.

'A sheep skeleton... We should've known, shouldn't we, Emer? Girls, huh.'

'I'm a girl.'

'I forgot.'

Relief mingled with the perspiration beading his forehead. He folded his knife and put it in his pocket.

'Let's go home, Emer. What d'ya say?'

'Yeah, let's.'

Then as strong as a touch her nostrils caught a rancid smell. It wasn't from the sheep's carcass. This was a stench of decay above that of a sheep long decomposed.

'Come on,' G.I. urged.

'Do you get a really bad smell?'

'It's not off me, so it's not.'

'I didn't say it was, did I?'

'No. I guess not.'

G.I. disappeared into the gorse. On her knees, and about to enter the furze tunnel, she cast a look to her right, her attention snared by the colours black and white, stark against the furze, partially obscured by a fringe of nettles. Staring at the soles of G.I.'s brandless trainers she backed out and walked over, eyes squinting. The source of the stench... she thought... *Leave it.*

The sacking covered a longish object bound with duct tape. Carpet, she thought, and then not, because she saw what looked like a sweater and a shirt through holes in the packaging. A sack full of rags, discarded by... See it. See it. See it – oh, Je – oh, feck. Glistening like a piece of Mam's freshly washed bone china set – a hand.

Retching – the taste of bile bitter in her mouth. Her stomach wanted to turn itself inside out. A bluebottle droned by her ear and she gave a weak flap of hand.

Emer sipped at her Napoleon brandy, struck up her Zippo and lit a cigar, shifted her memory on...

She'd disliked intensely the silence under the silence. The absence of birdsong. Wanted to hear the horses thundering on the gallops, hear a dog barking. Any noise that would break this awful silence – that silence with its revolting odour.

Wiping the corners of her mouth, she stepped back. The fly would not leave her alone. Nana once said the bluebottle was the devil's spy.

Think. Think, she had thought back then. She couldn't let G.I. see this. When Hannah returned the place would swarm with people, the guards, the news would break G.I.'s heart. He lived for his mother coming home.

'Emer, are you coming!' G.I.'s voice tremored with nervousness.

'Yeah, yes, I'm on my way. Wait.'

Dashing through the undergrowth, surfacing, she couldn't bring herself to face G.I.

'Girls,' G.I. breathed, 'wouldn't you just know it, wouldn't you?'

'Yeah, girls,' she said, 'I'm a—'

'Girl, yeah, but not a real one – has a boy ever kissed you?'

'Has one ever kissed you?'

'Don't be stupid.'

'Don't be stupid, you.'

'Gee, you look like you saw a ghost, Emer. Are you going to faint? Don't, won't you not, cos I'd have to do mouth-to-mouth stuff to save you, and that'd be Jesus-ing awful.'

'To tell you the truth I don't feel so good.'

She looked to the east where Hannah had run, to the road that merged with the plains.

Where are they? she thought. *Where is the help?*

Perhaps Hannah hadn't opened her mouth to speak. Perhaps she'd been stricken dumb.

She felt numb too. Shaky in herself. Tears queued to fall but she bit her hand a little to prevent the flow. She had to hold herself together for G.I.'s sake. She didn't want people who didn't know G.I. trampling all over him with bad news.

'We'll walk on a bit more, G.I... to the rath.'

'I don't know, Emer. I'm hungry.'

'You need the exercise.'

'I need food. I'm starving, so I am. Let's go home. Your mam might invite me in for chips.'

'Do you remember the guy who robbed all the Easter eggs?'

Prompt enough to soften G.I.'s resolve. A guy the guards called the Bunny thief was caught red handed with two sacks of pricey Easter eggs in a wheelbarrow. He'd robbed a lot of shops and hid most of his illicit gains in the furze bushes covering the ancient raths – embanked forts. She knew G.I. wouldn't suss the eggs would be long spoiled, and the likelihood of them being found was remote.

She had shuddered at a savage sweep of thought: what had been the odds of their finding G.I.'s mam?

A linnet swooped and dived as they approached the grassy embankment encircling tall, dense furze. The residence of pookas and leprechauns, her Nana had said.

She'd asked herself how she was going to tell G.I. his mother wasn't coming home. *Is it my job to let him know?* she'd thought. *Shouldn't his father break the news? His Aunt Tam? A priest – no, not a priest because G.I. isn't the sort who feels comfortable in a stranger's company.*

'When are we going to start looking for those eggs?' G.I. said. 'Eh, I hope we find them before the sheep do.'

'Sheep don't eat chocolate, G.I.'

'Emer, everyone eats chocolate.'

'Sheep aren't people.'

'If you're hungry you'd eat anything. People eat people, you know.'

'Jesus…'

Dragging her forearm across her nose she went to speak but the words hit a rock in her throat. These words managed to squeeze themselves beyond the rock. 'Ah, they could be anywhere, G.I.'

'This could be anywhere.'

'Well, it's not!' she snapped.

She noticed small dust clouds conjured by vehicles making to where G.I.'s mam lay wrapped in plastic packaging, watched over by the eye sockets of a dead sheep. She imagined Hannah's eyes hitting tissue, her directions interrupted by bouts of crying. She had a new memory. Unwanted. Emer wondered if G.I.'s father was among them. She wondered other things about him. Suspicions – fell as blood-red confetti.

'G.I.,' she said, in the air of a graveyard visit.

No reply.

He must be stung at the way she'd turned on him. Plus he got narky when hungry. She put her hand on his shoulder and turned him about to meet with her eyes.

Tears rolled along G.I.'s blubbery cheeks, silently bleeding from the heart.

'What's the matter, Emer, why are you mad at me?'

They were out of the cars now. She could distinguish Hannah, the navy uniforms of the guards.

'What's going on?' G.I. said, mopping his tears with the sleeve of his tracksuit. 'Why did Hannah bring the guards out here?'

She began. Each word caused breakage.

He backed away, hands cupping his ears, stomping his feet to the beat of high-pitched wailing. He would run from her, from the truth, if able.

She waited for him to quieten in the settling dust of awful news, in the rubble of his heart.

The western skies turned beautiful reds and ambers before they started for the cars down below. Her friend hadn't said a word since she'd told him. She thought he knew all along – that he'd sensed the truth, knew what was coming, and his soul had hidden it from him.

He was whiter than a sun-bleached Texas cow skull. He looked way out into the distance, at invisible things she realised even best friends were not allowed to see.

*

Wakened by the village minaret loudspeaking its call to prayer, Emer put her feet to the rug, yawned. Made her bunk. Folded the two-week-old newspaper from home, at the piece ringed by Hannah, concerning G.I.'s... Joe Divine's death in a single-vehicle car collision... News that had saddened Emer. They hadn't seen each other since that day on the Curragh... Life is full of roses and thorns. Her divorce was one, but when she returned from Ireland in a fortnight's time, it should be done and dusted, and she'd have one less thorn cutting at her. G.I. had left two kids behind, a wife. How old was he...? Thirty. Two years younger than her. Twenty years ago. Reading about his death was like having the coldest of shadows pass through her – the newspaper piece seemed to her to be a rubber stamping of a reality. When a death occurred old friendships took on a resurrection of sorts in the form of memories. Lived with her for a while until time cauterised the sorrow, and a faint pallor of healing began. *Whether you like it or not, Emer*, she thought, *times wears away at pain till you reach the coping layer.*

PART ONE

Nora tried to stand but waves of pain crushed her feeble attempt. She was too dizzy, too sickened, in far too much distress. Instead, wheezing hard, she lay back down.

The kindness of a breeze touched.

The dark night stood almost still. There were stars, a slice of the moon. Close-by palm trees rustled and perhaps there was a scent of burning sage. Or maybe not, she thought. More like tobacco from a hookah wafting to her nostrils. Bloodied nostrils. Apple. Yes, more like the sap of apple-flavoured tobacco.

Where am I? God... the pain...

A memory found a clearing in the miasma; the nightclub, their accusations, his fist catching her under her eye. Jenny running, running away. Leaving her alone with *him*. To deal with him by herself.

She called out as loudly as she could, 'Help...' but it was the whimpering croak of a badly hurt animal.

The stillness was broken by slow and ponderous shuffling movements. It puzzled her.

A face loomed close to her slightly blurred vision. The old man said something in Arabic to another behind him. His blue-grey eyes were wide in shock as he gently touched her shoulder. She felt herself beginning again to shut down; she closed the small slits of her eyes to the world.

Gone now to a place where the pain could not reach her.

CHAPTER 1

'Sir,' Emer said, flummoxed, trying vainly to get a handle on the right response, 'you can't be serious. Really?'

She stared across the desk at her commanding officer, a man in his early sixties. There was no softness in his expression. His blue eyes held the steady glow of a Norwegian sun settling on dawn frost.

This is a wind-up, she thought, crossing her legs, her hand squeezing her blue beret.

'Is there a problem?' he said.

'Sir. You know the problem. You're aware that I'm going on leave tomorrow, for two weeks. I... and...'

He joined his fingertips and sniffled, looked at the wall calendar, then back at her.

Emer said quietly, 'I'm also the company's administration officer, sir. My job is dealing with pay and leave and the detachments, transport documentation, all of that.'

'You're needed here, for now.'

'Sir.'

He went on, 'You are firstly a military police officer and I read in your file that you were once with the Irish civilian police. You have had some investigative training and experience. Yes?'

'Yes. But—'

'Good.'

A dull pain began to flare in her forehead. She had spent two months in south Lebanon, at the UN Headquarters, as part of the international military police company – a.k.a. MP Coy – with a cushy working routine; a beach literally a stone's throw away, most weekends off and a quitting time of 3 pm.

He sighed and held out his hands in a parody of them being tied, and said, 'This is an Irish case and your senior Irish officer in Headquarters has demanded an Irish involvement. As you know, the Irish investigator had to be sent home for compassionate reasons...' Colonel Fredericksen shrugged and continued. 'Morris, the Irish senior officer, is not an easy man to deal with it. You know him, of course.'

She nodded.

Laughter exploded outside, a burst of greetings between passing Fijian and Nepalese military police. Across from the military police camp a helicopter began to rotate its blades in the Italair compound. The Huey would fly directly overhead, shaking the windows, drowning out voices, veer right and head north along the coastal road to Beirut. Here, south Lebanon resembled the fields of the west of Ireland, with its bony spines segregating fields. It shared that same sense of isolation, abandonment, a backyard left to itself.

Fredericksen left his seat to close the window. A ceiling fan moved lethargically, almost uselessly. Emer touched the fob on her shirt pocket, crossed flintlocks on a red background, and brought her eyes to the calendar on the Formica wall – it had a photograph of demining personnel sweeping a dirt-track under the ruins of a Crusader castle in the mountain village of Tibnin. All dates crossed except today's: June 10th, 2010.

After returning to his desk, Fredericksen said, 'This is our world.'

She bit on her lower lip. *Sir*, she thought, *you don't know John Moore. John's diary allows for none of his days being wasted. His, that is. Mine are a different matter.*

'Sir, it's taken my ex and I two years to finally get around to fixing this date,' she said.

He shrugged and said, 'Lieutenant Timo Lahr from the SIS has also been assigned to the case.'

This, she told herself, *just keeps getting worse.* She couldn't swear to it, but at a crowded event last month he was her prime suspect for patting her ass as he passed her. If she'd known for sure, she'd have clocked him on the spot.

'He's a rank below mine,' she said, beginning to bristle.

'He's the Officer in Charge of the Special Investigation Section, yes?'

'Hmm.'

'And he is Finnish civil police, a professional police officer, and so is more suitably qualified to lead the investigation.'

'A rank below mine,' she reiterated.

'He will brief you on the case – I am surprised that you did not ask me what it is.'

'I'm still in shock. I wasn't expecting to hear any of this.'

'Go and have some coffee in the mess and gather yourself together.'

Silence as the heli passed over, shaking all, in harmony with the dance of Emer's suppressed anger.

She brought her mug of coffee to a table under a bamboo awning at the rear of the mess, the military police club. The wide balcony overlooked the rocky shore and the glinting Mediterranean. A good distance out from shore, Israeli patrol vessels passed each other. She brought her Zippo to her thin cigar and lit up; inhaled and exhaled, took some coffee, thinking she would pop down to the gym later and pound the stuffing out of the bag. But first she would have to break the news to John. Her stomach was sick at the thought of telling him. She asked herself why. After all, they were long done with each other. Her concern about what he might say, surprised her. She thought it strange. She'd been looking forward to severing the ties. Getting that fresh start. *Don't go excavating feelings and emotions now*, she thought.

Done that. Move on. But...

John Moore, 34.

Four years married. A marriage more often on the rocks than peacefully drifting in the waters. Always in her ear to leave that stupid poxy job. *Army? What army? Who needs an army? Waste of bloody taxpayers' money.* He said the country needed an auxiliary police force, not a lame-duck sham army. When she had told him why she wanted to hold on to her job, he fell quiet; he wasn't taking in what she had said; he was just screening out her reason, like it wasn't worthy of an answer or further discussion. Marriage – a long-time creaking before the hinges finally gave.

He hadn't shown that side to himself before they were married. They'd met at a rugby club do and later in the same week at an art exhibition where Hannah had a painting displayed. He bought it for a nice sum, 350 euros. He had a generous side to him and at times still had, but the more money he seemed to get, the more he seemed reluctant to part with it – and especially when he bought several properties cheaply in the crash and let them back into the market at triple their former rent. He hired a property manager to keep his tenants distant from him; he didn't want to know if they lost jobs, had bereavements – had real reasons for missing on paying the rent. She understood business was business, but she began less and less to like the cutting side to his soul. And when he sneered as she spilled tears looking at a dead child washed up on a Greek beach on TV, and tried to qualify it by saying his parents should be shot for child neglect, she knew that the fault line between them was increasing. She'd asked him, 'John, where has the real you gotten to? Tell me?'

A shadow fell across the ochre floor, and she turned her head. Lahr stood in the doorway, hand on the frame.

'Captain Harte, this is where you are,' he said, his accent coarse, delivery robotic. Typical Finnish.

He moved to the wicker armchair opposite her, slouching into it. Staring disapprovingly at the half cigar in the ashtray, he said, 'I like cigars. You shouldn't smoke poor quality... Here... have a Cuban.'

He brought it up a little from his shirt pocket, half certain she would shake her head.

She declined, and said, 'I—'

'I heard about your holiday plans.'

His sympathetic tone made the lump in her throat grow, and she felt the tightening of the knot in her stomach.

She sipped at her coffee, aware he was coolly appraising her.

Though she thought she had a goodish figure, she always felt self-conscious in Lahr's presence. It was that look he had, raising his nose a little like his eyes had given him a sense of something slightly off. Boxing scars across her cheekbone and forehead, the badly reset broken nose. God knows what he made of those.

Her short auburn hair, boyish. John had said she looked like an overgrown tomboy.

Lahr said quietly, 'I can brief you on the way to Jerusalem. You should go pack a bag.'

'First, I have a couple of calls to make.'

He nodded and said he would wait for her in the MP car park.

She thought to relay the news through the solicitor handling the divorce. But it was better to keep things amicable as possible with John.

Okay. Deep breath. In. Out. Ring.

'You've got to be kidding me, Emer,' he said. 'We've had the date set for months.'

A stream of invectives poured from him.

Silence.

She said, 'You're finished with the rant, good. I could have had my lawyer call to tell yours.'

Another silence.

'John?' she said.

He'd hung up.

The little F'r.

Next, she rang the solicitor.

Then her sister, Hannah, but she killed the call before it connected.

Speaking to John and the solicitor had left her feeling upset and frustrated, and Hannah would only add a real pinch of sadness to an already painful mix.

She passed a line of MP vehicles and glimpsed through a window in the Duty Room; Lahr was making a call. Emer's quarters were in the first row of a complex of prefabs on the hill, just behind the whitewashed edifice that was adorned in large black letters United Nations Interim Force in Lebanon, Headquarters.

Some interim, she thought. *Twenty-eight years and counting since the peacekeepers arrived.*

She took the steps two at a time, continued along the asphalt path, and smelled the roses under the windows of her room as she let herself in. Their perfume reminded her to water the bonsai plant on her desk. She packed her green travel bag quickly, threw some loose shekels into its side pocket, and left. As she walked, John's vicious reaction circled inside her head. He'd no business speaking to her like that. No, she wasn't playing mind games and punishing him – when had she ever bloody done that to him? Eejit.

Almost from the beginning her army career had been a major sticking point. He could not get how much it mattered. To have her own position, her own money – when he could afford for her to not work at all. Emer remembered her mother working two jobs to support Hannah and her, always watching the money. Their father too spiteful, too tight to part with money after she had left him. He was loaded and almost seemed to enjoy making her beg for cash to fund their daughters' school trips and special occasions.

No man was going to make her depend on him for money, she thought.

Ever.

Punish him?

For what?

Untying the knots in her stomach?

Hannah advised her to give it another go. Gave a small snort when told it'd be easier to iron away a camel's hump.

CHAPTER 2

Lahr was behind the wheel, waiting for her in the car park in a Toyota Landcruiser, its engine purring, windows closed. She threw her bag on the back seat and sat up front.

'You're sure that you don't mind driving?' she said with an edge.

'I'm used to driving in Israel. Are you?' he replied with a smile he probably thought disarming but she considered otherwise.

'Just drive,' she said.

They eased left onto the major camp road, passed the Muslim cemetery and its Moorish keep, Polish Logistics, the French infantry base, travelling 2 km before exiting the UN base onto the coastal road, southwards. On their right, the Mediterranean and the iron skeleton of a railway line that war had destroyed, and peace did not see the sense in repairing. To the left, those Connemara hills, grassy patches, goats, and cows with sunken-in flanks.

She lowered the A/C current.

Lahr said, 'Are you ready to hear the details?'

'I've got nothing else to do for the next couple of hours, I suppose.'

His eyes – well, she thought they were scrutinising her scars and her nose and said, 'What?'

'Your scars. That one above your eyebrow.'

'You're very pass remarkable.'

'What does that mean?'

'Do you have to make a comment? Would you say something like that to a person in a wheelchair? No, I doubt it.'

'This is different. I have a dog with a scar the exact same. I will show you the photo on my phone, later.'

'I can't believe you said that.'

'Her name is Swan and she is a labrador.'

'I'm thrilled for you. I wouldn't be too happy for the dog, though, having you as an owner. Swan... What a name for a dog.'

'You are a boxer,' he remarked.

She found no sarcasm in his tone... Not a hint of it, despite his dog references, and said, 'Was. Who told you?'

'I heard it from one of the Irish.'

'Gossips.'

'You were not a good one,' he said, looking at her and using his thumb to press on his nose a little. He laughed, not in a cruel way, but just about keeping to the edge of banter.

'I broke my nose and got the bad scar in a car accident,' she said. 'I couldn't box after that.'

'Oh... oh.'

She recalled the dark and wet winter's evening and the speed her then-boyfriend was doing around the bend, how the electricity pole seemed to grow huge all of a sudden. Afterwards, his main concern was about how much his insurance would climb if she claimed for compensation. He said it a few times until she told him to shut up. Such a dickhead. She didn't file a claim. Emer was happy just to have survived and to have discovered that her boyfriend was shallower than shallow before things got too serious between them.

'Two Irish female soldiers have gone missing,' he said, kicking dust over her memory.

He paused to let the news take root with her.

'Go on,' she said, the seriousness of the fact biting at her.

'Their names are on the clipboard in my bag,' he said, hiking his

21

thumb over his shoulder.

'I can read it from here.'

'Listen,' he said, suddenly losing the softness to his tone and features, 'can you stop being the funny woman?'

'Funny?'

'Uncooperative.'

'Oh, so your calling me a dog wasn't being funny.'

'I didn't call you a dog.'

'No, but you said your dog looked like me. It's the same thing, really.'

He hadn't, she knew, but she wanted to mess with him a little.

'No,' he said, 'I have a picture and I—'

'Ah, shove it.'

'Who else could they send? Tell me?' he said, his wrists guiding the steering wheel, his finger counting off on the free hand. 'Nepalese, Fijian, Ghanaian, Polish. Do you think the Ghanaians or the Nepalese would be capable of investigating this case, do you? How about Chief Joseph?'

The Fijian officer who was quite literally a chief, farmer, and a police officer at home in Suva. Laidback and lazy, for sure. Charismatic, too.

Coming up to a large pothole, he fixed his hands to the wheel and eased through.

Colour, too, she understood, played a role in the dynamics within the MP camp. Scandinavians held their non-white colleagues in some disdain – so too did some of the Irish, the French and the Italians. She recognised the sad gulf with telescopic clarity, for it was a first cousin of the sort occasionally displayed toward women. Not that this attitude confined itself to the UN but was also found in the Arab world outside the camp, where men did not like to learn that a woman had more brain power than several of their own combined.

Though it was no boast for a woman to publicly assert the fact.

Emer was not the only woman in the 53-strong MP company; there were two drug dog-handlers and a Transport NCO. But she was the sole female officer.

'We need to be bearing down on this ASAP, Lahr,' Emer said as they reached the border crossing. 'They might hurry us through if you explain why we're in a rush.'

'I will ask.'

But his enquiry did not smooth their passage. A contrary-looking sentry ushered them into an inspection bay for the Israeli mechanics to carry out a search. Then they crossed the road to the terminal to pass through the X-ray machine and have their bags checked by an MP, under the watchful eye of an Israeli customs official.

Lebanon and Israel: neighbours itching to rip the hearts out of each other's souls. It had been that way for almost 70 years, ever since the Jews ousted Palestine from the world map. The majority of Palestinians fled into neighbouring Arab countries, like Lebanon and Jordan. The Irish had been involved in trying to factor a permanent peace into the area with their troops stationed in the hills of Lebanon for decades. Some 47 Irish soldiers had died while on service and the roll call of UNIFIL's fallen tallied into the hundreds, making for sombre reading on the marble commemoration stone. Those names unsettled her, when she thought of the families behind each one, the children left bereft at the loss.

Once over the border, Lahr said he was hungry and pulled into a roadside café. Next to it was an office offering cable cars to the sea caves underneath. Emer had never visited; she did not trust funiculars.

'I think we should keep going. Grab yourself a banana or something,' she said.

He wasn't listening, the car door already closing behind him.

She went to the bathroom while Lahr joined the queue. Her

stomach was sour with the bad news that had yet to be fully digested. Jerusalem. Not Dublin. She'd been to the MP detachments in Israel: Jerusalem, Metula and Netanya and to the two in Lebanon; Tyre and Beirut – routine visits to check on the cleanliness of the rented buildings, to sort leave and pay matters, general detachment administration. Keep the crew on their toes, Fredericksen had said. All the more since several military police had been out partying instead of attending a fatal car crash involving a UN vehicle. Heads rolled in the aftermath in the form of demotions and repatriation; Fredericksen did not like to be looked at in a bad light.

Crossing the border was like leaving the wilds of Atlantic Ireland behind and rolling into Gran Canaria or some other resort. Here, everything was clean; the roads had no pockmarks, traffic lights worked. This was civilisation – south Lebanon, the jungle. The air tasted differently; the energy was more vibrant. Perhaps Lebanon would be like this if its neighbour had not bludgeoned the soul out of it, she thought.

The aroma of food on the grill made her feel hungry. She ordered scrambled eggs and toast, a pot of tea, and brought her tray to the panoramic window where Lahr was seated. The clipboard was on the table.

Stirring the tea in the pot, then squeezing the bag against its side, she said, 'What would you do if your leave were cancelled at the last second? What would your wife say?'

He sipped at his black coffee, cut through an egg sandwich with a plastic knife. Sunglasses perched above a clear forehead and fair mono eyebrow. Chewed his food as he said, 'Nothing.'

'Really,' she said.

'I don't have a wife.'

'Divorced?'

'She's dead.'

He drew his fingertip down a coffee slick on his mug and wiped it in a napkin.

'I'm sorry,' she said.

'I think she would have gone crazy if I had to tell her news like yours.'

'What was it?' she said.

'Cancer.'

'That's tough. I'm sorry.'

'I have a daughter, Jacki. She is six. Here,' he said, bringing up a photo on his phone.

'Oh, she's absolutely beautiful.'

A flow of blonde hair, a broad smile, gorgeous blue eyes. Thin, though; very thin.

'She's not well,' he said, his voice riding over a cough. 'It is hereditary, like her mother.'

'Oh, I'm sorry,' she said, wondering what had him here, if his daughter was ill. Shouldn't he be with her? The poor mite had lost her mother. Why would he run the risk of being in a war zone?

'This is my dog,' he said, moving on quickly to the next picture.

Yeah, the scar… It did resemble hers. A little. 'Nice looking dog,' she said.

'She is, yes.'

'I have to ask you, Lahr, what are you doing here, if your daughter isn't well?'

'Money,' he said. 'She needs an operation and follow-on treatment next year, and,' he sighed, 'it's how it is. I get more than double here with allowances. She's staying with my mother at her apartment in Helsinki, so I know she is being well cared for – that gives me some peace of mind.'

He set to refilling his mug, with eyes suggestive of his soul feeling left out of something.

'You know,' she said, picking up a slice of her toast, simultaneously reaching for the clipboard, 'I'm okay to have a good look at this now.'

CHAPTER 3

She skimmed her eyes over the erratically hand-written details, penned on UN-headed notepaper: blue laurel leaves cupping a blue globe. A UN tour bus left UN HQ six days ago – 04 June, with 15 personnel on board: 6 Irish, 3 Fijian, 2 Polish (including the driver) and 4 French. Four females, all Irish. The itinerary: Akko, Metula, Mount of Beatitudes, Tiberias, Nazareth, Netanya, Tel Aviv, Jerusalem, Bethlehem. All personnel were normally based in Naqoura, UN Headquarters.

On 8 June, two days ago, two Irish female soldiers were reported missing, after attending a nightclub in Jerusalem. Corporal Nora Sexton and Private Jenny Casey. Both aged 24. Emer studied the names on the list. The Officer in Charge of the tour was Captain Myles O'Rourke. She knew Myles. Easy-going. Grounded, she would also have said. A couple of weeks ago, she'd attended a history lecture he'd given about the Holy Land. He used a film projector to show the important sites, and jokingly advised his small audience not to buy so-called Phoenician and Roman coins from traders in the souks, saying his mother-in-law was older than that sort of currency.

'Is this it?' she said, waving the paper. 'Everything we know, really?'

'That's the information I received. There's a contact number on the back for O'Rourke and the address of the Pilgrim Hotel, where the group is staying. I've been in touch with Benny at the detachment in Jerusalem. He's going to call to the hotel. I spoke to O'Rourke too and told him that no one was to leave the hotel.'

'Good. But two days ago. Why are we only being told now? This is crazy. When did we receive notification?'

'Seven a.m. This morning.'

Her phone sounded. An unknown number.

'Hello,' she said.

'Colonel Morris here. Captain Harte?'

'Sir.'

'You're en route?'

'Yes.'

'Okay, first off – you are to report your findings on these absentees to me directly, before reporting to anyone else.'

A big ask. And putting her in the firing line. Fredericksen was her commanding officer and had first call on her loyalty. Morris was only too aware of this.

'With due respect, sir, Colonel Fredericksen expects that of me, too. But Lieutenant Lahr is the lead investigator and I'll talk to him about it.'

'I've just given you an order.'

'Which I think would be classed as an unlawful one.'

'Listen, Captain. Who do you think will write up your overseas performance report at the end of your tour of duty?'

He was niggling her and a profanity came to mind, but she resolved not to give him leverage to hold a charge of insubordination over her.

'Sir,' she said evenly, 'but your report might conflict with the excellent report my MP officer will issue me with, for certain. Then, you'll have questions to answer.'

She gave her phone the middle finger.

'That's if he gives you one. I want this sorted quickly. I'm ordering you to have both of those soldiers standing in front of my desk by tomorrow evening.'

'I'll most certainly do my best to comply with your instructions, sir.'

This man's got pebbles for brains.

'Colonel Morris. You are aware that they've been missing for two days. How long have you known that?'

No answer.

'Colonel Morris?'

Has he hung up?

'Colonel Morris?'

He has.

A sigh left her like a slow puncture.

'What is the matter?' Lahr asked quietly.

'That was Colonel Gerry Morris, the senior Irish officer at HQ – he wants to be kept up to date about the case and wants to see the girls tomorrow evening.'

Lahr chuckled, canted his head, then shook it.

'No problem,' he said. 'Tell him what he thinks is new news but is really a little old.'

'Hmm.'

We Irish, she thought, *have a thing when it comes to our own making them look bad in front of the neighbours.* This 'thing' was magnified 100 times in an international environment. Morris was wrong in another regard: the soldiers couldn't be classed as absentees as they were on leave. Leave that was due to end tomorrow. *Two days missing, and we hear of it this morning. My god. Remote jungle drums would ferry news quicker.*

Lahr said, 'I want you to know something.'

'What?'

'It is my experience, yes? Some cases, even the bad ones, I don't get a bad feeling for. Some, I do.'

'You have a bad feeling about this. Is that what you're saying?'

29

'Yes.'

She got the impression that he had more to tell her – comparable to some conversations she had had with John; she'd sense he was holding back, as though he dreaded her reaction, knew it and feared it.

CHAPTER 4

Lahr eased the Landcruiser into a space at the detachment in Jerusalem, next to a military police patrol vehicle. He took the vehicle's logbook from the glove compartment, opened its thick hessian cover that had the registration number stencilled in black. Emer watched as he went through the drill of reading and recording the mileage. She wondered if he did this because of the sharp words she had exchanged a while back with a couple of his staff, for not complying with transport rules.

'We might be going out later,' she said, 'so maybe you shouldn't fill it out until you've finished driving for the day.'

'No, we'll have the Jerusalem MPs bring us to the hotel,' he said, snapping the cover shut and putting it away.

'Fine,' Emer said.

A Nepalese sergeant greeted them at the small reception desk, saluting and smiling, saying, 'Welcome, ram ram.'

He lifted the flyleaf and ushered them through into a kitchen and dining area.

Lahr asked, 'Where is Dogface?' The nickname or codename for the detachment commander.

'He is in hospital.'

'Tell him that we are here,' Lahr said, sitting to the table.

'Yes, yes, he is in hospital.'

Lahr sighed and looked across at Emer, who smiled.

Slowly, she addressed Pedney, looking at his nametag. 'Is there anyone else here?'

'Yes, in hospital… I make tea, coffee… Y'all like coffee?'

How he had said it, with a thick Mississippi accent, brought smiles to the officers.

In the rising song of the electric kettle, they heard a vehicle pull up outside.

Pedney said, as he washed cups under the tap, 'He no in hospital now, he back.'

Dogface was a Polish staff sergeant by the name of Benny Rafal. Broad-shouldered, he was tall with a link chain tattooed in blue around his left wrist. Emer thought it something more appropriate for an ex-con than an MP.

'You were at the hospital,' Lahr said drily. 'Pedney told us.'

'Yes, I was speaking with Sexton, the corporal.'

Emer stared at Lahr, her mouth open, and then said in astonishment, 'She's – she was found?'

'Of course, I say you she is in hospital. That's why I was there. Pedney, he did not tell you?'

'No,' replied Emer, 'I thought it was for something routine, to pick up a med report from a traffic accident, the usual.'

Lahr said into the quietness, 'Is she okay?'

Rafal shook his head, moved his lips. 'She has swelled face, missing teeth – she looks bad, but the doctor say she will be okay in a few weeks.'

Emer pressed, 'Did she say anything?'

'She tried. But I could not hear her, and the doctor say she must rest. No more questions.'

'The other soldier,' Lahr queried.

'Missing.'

'Where was Sexton found?' Emer said.

'At the Mount of Olives in the early morning, by a man who was bringing his camel there for the tourists in the early morning. He saw her lying beside a garbage bin. I have his name; the Israel police give it.'

'Good,' Lahr said.

'We take a little break, get something to eat?' Rafal said. 'Then we go to hotel to see the people, yes?'

Emer brought her coffee outside and lit up a cigar. It was dark, the skies rich with stars. The detachment situated in the city suburbs was an ideal place from which to patrol the areas most visited by UN personnel on leave. Operations had wanted to withdraw the MP presence, citing the lack of incidents involving UN personnel. Fredericksen countered, saying it proved the MP presence was a positive influence; the reality was that nothing happened for an age, and then a series of incidents occurred at once; a car accident, a theft, burgled hotel room, a drunken altercation among UN soldiers or between the soldiers and the locals, and sometimes even with the police. But nothing like this had happened before.

Jerusalem.

She'd read with interest somewhere – either in the *National Geographic* or *The Lonely Planet* about a phenomenon called The Jerusalem Syndrome, which affected some 200 foreign tourists every year. Each so over-wrought at visiting the holy city and by its sacred locations that they became delusional and believed they were the reincarnation of Jesus or his mother or some saint. Never Judas, though. Or Caiaphas. Or Pilate. Frequently, the lights blew in their head at one of the revered sites and they set to lambasting 'sinners', smashing lamps and knocking over candelabra. It took a week of treatment in the state's psychiatric hospital at Kfar Shaul on the outskirts of West Jerusalem to rewire the patient. Not a new syndrome either, as in the 1930s an English Christian woman was so convinced that the arrival of Christ was imminent that she would regularly climb Mt Scopus to welcome Him back to Earth with a cup of tea. People sometimes accused another delusional John the Baptist of being an imposter.

Hannah, she suddenly thought. *I have to make that call.*

Emer finished her coffee and drew hard on her cigar before ringing her sister. The call went to voicemail and she left a brief message to say she'd call her in a day or so. She injected a brevity into her tone that she did not feel. Hannah was the one person who easily saw through such subterfuge. Emer was disappointed not to have heard her younger sister's comforting voice. She put her phone in her cargo pants' left pocket and buttoned the flap. She brought her thoughts to the case, the amazing news that Sexton was safe. Good news. But what of Jenny Casey?

Focus! She demanded of herself.

On the way to the hotel, Lahr asked her, 'How is your room at the Det?'

'Fine, Chief Joseph is on leave – I'm in his room and it's spick and span.'

She saw Benn Rafal study her in the rear-view mirror.

He said, 'He is a real chief, you know this, and a kava farmer?'

'Yes,' she said, 'he told me.'

In fact, they had had a couple of conversations in the MP mess, each easy in the other's company. Joseph had a genial nature with everyone.

'You're lucky,' Lahr said. 'I am sharing with Pedney and his statues of deities – I think he has one for every day of the year.'

'That would be hell for an atheist. You're not atheist, are you?' she said.

Silence spoke for him. 'Agnostic,' he then added.

*

Emer and the others waited in the hotel's lobby for the group to come from their rooms. Their arrival was staggered and a few had gone out. They sat on plush sofas around mosaic-layered coffee tables.

'Gone out,' Emer said with quiet annoyance to Myles O'Rourke. 'You were instructed to have everyone present.'

O'Rourke was a gangly man with reddish hair. A man who knew the Holy Land, its history, old and new, who warned people against buying dodgy antique coins.

'They were told,' his tone laced with frustration. 'I suspect they went to the hospital to visit Corporal Sexton.'

'Have them report here... Now,' she said.

'I've tried, but they're not answering their phones.'

'Tell me, Myles, who reported the girls as missing?'

'I did.'

'Why the delay?'

'This sort of thing has happened before, with the guys too; they would go on a bender and not show up for two to three days.'

'On other tours, you mean, people went missing. Unreported absences?'

The question threw him a little because he hesitated before saying, 'They just want to let off steam when they cross the border, sometimes. I cut them some slack, that's all.'

She went to say something but withheld her words. The man was clearly suffering; upset and ashamed. Worried. It wasn't usual for Irish soldiers to disobey an order, lawful or otherwise; O'Rourke's charges appeared to have no problem when it came to flouting them.

Why would they do that? Why would they risk blotting their record? Did they not respect O'Rourke? Or had they something on him that disabled any threat? Or did they view him as being cushy, more friend than their superior officer?

'Okay, Myles,' Emer said, looking at the inventory he had handed her, a list of names with their units, ages, ranks, the day and time they crossed the border.

Absent were the Polish driver, an Irish quartermaster and two of the remaining Irish girls. Everyone else was accounted for, and their statements recorded over the course of two hours. Emer tallied up five statements and each was a vacuum; none had been at the club on the night in question and hadn't mingled much with Casey and Sexton. There wasn't any discord within the touring party or at least none that was noticed. It was as though, Emer thought, they had been handed the same hymn sheet. If ten people witness a traffic accident, the statements would each read differently; not everything would match. So, this stank and worryingly.

What are they hiding? Have they lied out of fear? Or self-preservation? Both?

Clues. Only in the aftermath of an event do people recognise them as being such. How often do people see the clues after a tragedy and not before? Her thoughts turned to the matching statements; the paucity of information rankled.

'So, we've got to interview how many more?' Lahr said.

'Four,' Emer said.

Benny said, 'Those who have gone to see Casey, yes?'

Emer nodded. 'Those are her best pals, maybe.'

'It's Sexton,' Lahr reminded. 'Casey is the one who is missing.'

Emer sighed, 'Casey.'

'The Irish captain,' Lahr said to Emer, 'he is under a lot of pressure.'

*

'Of course, he's bound to be. It's a big feather in an officer's cap, something to be proud of, if he brings everyone home from a dangerous overseas mission – and he's lost one while on bloody holiday. And some of this party – they have to be across the border tomorrow as they're needed for duties back at base.'

'They can go, after we interview the remaining ones,' Lahr said.

He looked at his watch. 'We are not waiting any longer for them.'

As they rose, Benny remained seated and said dejectedly, 'I have one thing.'

He appeared to be speaking to the black lining in his blue beret. His mood was low.

'The Polish warrant officer I interviewed… His name is Janus Dabrowski and the driver is his younger brother, Lukas.'

'What about them?' Emer said, sitting back down.

Lahr remained standing.

'They are Polish mafia.'

Here, serving with the United Nations? Emer asked herself.

'They are dangerous men,' he said gravely, 'and during the interview, he said I could get to know your family.'

Emer pondered if the threat was reinforced with a demonstration of violence.

Lahr said, slowly nodding his head, 'I will interview the driver tomorrow and you can interpret.'

'I do not have to – his English is very good.'

As they made their way to the patrol car, her phone sounded its 7th Cavalry bugle charge. Unknown number. Hmm. She guessed it was Colonel Gerry Morris and didn't answer.

Her thoughts were deep on Benny Rafal's revelation.

She'd read something in his facial expression, as though he'd divulged a fact that would have emerged as the case progressed, so better to admit it now.

What was it, though? A distancing of himself from a situation or someone?

Am I reading things correctly?

Benny Rafal did not fully convince her, for whatever reason. His words sang like a bell without a gong. Nor was she convinced by Myles O'Rourke, the coin-man. Just something about them, something that wasn't right.

CHAPTER 5

They drove in silence, travelling in heavy traffic. A little after 8 pm. Emer recalled her first visit to Jerusalem, a couple of days after she'd touched ground in the Levant – taking in quick trips to the Church of the Holy Sepulchre, King David's Tomb, the Mount of Olives. She was raised as a Catholic but undid the shackles of that faith when she turned 16, much to the consternation of her poor late mother who was a true believer, always in search of a cross to nail herself and someone else to. Her father had believed tacitly, for the time he was with her, for the sake of peace, to keep himself from being nailed to a cross – now in Heaven, so Hannah liked to say. In many ways her mother's daughter. Probably the very type who would scale a mountain to bring Jesus a cup of tea.

Emer remembered her mother making the sign of the cross several times, after hearing her daughter declare herself an atheist. All those times in church, she'd never felt at ease in a place where women didn't have equal status. It was a men's club and had more rules than oats in a bag of porridge; a rule that could be undone by another rule. And she chose not to abide by them. No major event, no sickening child sexual abuse scandal had influenced her beliefs – they had been solid before that cancer became frequent news.

Benny said in a disappointed tone, as though he had little to look forward to in life, 'Pedney is cooking.'

After a quick shower, she hurried unnoticed from the shower room with a Shamrock Rovers bath towel wrapped around her body. She dried off in Chief Joseph's bedroom.

Clean white linen sheets, plump pillows with cream slips. Photographs of his wife and son, standing alongside him, on his bedside locker. In the background a stand of trees with serrated leaves, a patch of sea. A tall man, well built, with shovel-sized hands that had callouses. The trio were smiling. He was away from them for one year. Too long for a family to be apart. On an earlier visit, he had said such a lengthy separation ruined many marriages and relationships. He did not mean his own, she had thought, but he hadn't said, so she could only assume.

She'd liked the kava he'd given her to sample. It tasted of washed earth and had a mildly narcotic effect. Good for the eyes, he said, and she found that it was. It felt as though her sockets had been cleansed from the inside out. He asked if she was happy being single, not having a man in her life. She shrugged, which, he pointed out, was not an answer. Then, Lahr arrived to speak with him and they never picked up on the threads of the conversation.

A sudden feeling of loneliness speared her heart. She'd wanted a child with John, when he'd mattered to her, and she to him. There was no happy and smiling family portrait on her bedside locker in UN Headquarters. If she'd had a child, would things have panned out differently with John? She doubted it. What she had witnessed among her older friends, was their children maturing to become strangers.

Would I have wanted to rear a child with a self-centred tosser for a father?

Think about something else, she told herself.

Food. I'm starving.

Dinner?

A combination of boiled cabbage and alleged chicken pieces, with a bowl of yellow rice and a plate of thinly sliced brown bread.

Poor fare, she thought as she picked at a chicken leg, sticking mainly to the rice. Noticed Lahr getting stuck into the meal. Such was his resolve, she believed he would devour it even if it meant he'd to spit out feathers.

Later, in the small sitting room, Benny opened bottles of lager with his eye-tooth and passed them around. She wore a loose white T-shirt that fell in line with the hemline of her blue shorts, which made it appear as though she were wearing a mini. Only Pedney openly stared at her, not just with his eyes but with his huge smile, like he was a prowling cat come across a bowl of milk it was not expecting to encounter on its route.

Benny slapped him playfully across the back of the head and gestured for him to leave the room.

'He is getting excited,' Benny explained.

As if she hadn't noticed.

Lahr, who had been dozing, said, 'What?'

Benny replied, eyes on the TV and the resumption of a Bayern Munich game, 'Pedney wants to fuck the Madam.'

Time to stamp on this.

'You like Pedney, Madam?' Benny said, chuckling.

'Watch the match, Staff Sergeant. Unless you would prefer to arrest Pedney for gross indecency. Right now, I have no idea what you mean by your saying he's excited.'

Men, she thought – they hone a woman's intuition until they can hear grass growing and their skin crawling.

CHAPTER 6

'Phone for you,' Lahr said when Emer was cracking a boiled egg for breakfast.

She went to the reception desk and picked the receiver up and said, 'Hello?'

'What were your instructions, Captain Harte?'

His words sharp and succinct.

Morris.

'To report to you, sir.'

'And why didn't you?'

'I was going to brief you later, after I'd spoken to Sexton, when I had formed a clearer picture of events.'

'You didn't think it important to tell me that one of the girls was found and is in hospital. I had to learn that from Fredericksen.'

Eh, he is my boss, she told herself.

'In addition, the Chief of Staff back home rang me to find out what's happening on the ground, and why he had to fecking well learn of the events in the *Irish Independent*.'

'Sir. Did he also want to know why it took two days for the matter to be reported to the MPs?'

'I'm sure you'll find the reason,' he said. 'She must know where Casey is and what happened.'

'I hope so.'

'Ring me this evening, at five, with a complete update. No later.'

Click. His words fell so hard they echoed for seconds inside her skull, chased by some of her own unvoiced responses.

Emer and Lahr were shown to a waiting room on the third floor and instructed to await the doctor's arrival. They sat next to each other on grey polypropylene chairs. Lahr sat with his legs extended, ankles crossed, while hers were drawn up and on the balls of her feet. The monkeys in her brain were having a tea party; those stupid girls, down from the theatre of operations and thinking they were in swinging Dublin. Or hi-jinking at the Irish Derby Festival at the Curragh Racecourse.

When the doctor, a short, handsome man, soft-faced, opened the door, they stood. He beckoned them into the corridor, away from the few people in the waiting room. After introductions, he said, 'The patient is in good health, considering. There are some deep cuts to her face and she has a badly swollen lower lip. Her left eye is closed and some hair has been pulled from her scalp. She is in a lot of pain. She lost some teeth and—'

'Can we speak to her?' Emer asked.

'Perhaps one of you can go in but do not stay for too long.'

Lahr said, 'Can we have her clothes, shoes, anything she came in with?'

'The police would have taken those, I'm sure,' the doctor said, 'but I will check for you.'

Emer said, 'Has she got her phone?'

'I don't think so,' he replied.

'I'll see her,' Emer said.

'And you come with me,' the doctor said to Lahr, 'and I will check on her belongings for you.'

'Did she have any visitors yesterday?' Emer asked.

'Again,' the doctor smiled, 'I think not, but I would need to confirm this.'

The men started to walk away, and then the doctor swivelled on his heel, his hand raised as though he had just snared a butterfly.

'Oh, one thing more,' he said.

'Yes,' she said.

'Normally, I wouldn't tell you, in respect of patient confidentiality, but it may help with the investigation and finding the animal who did this. And it can't be a hidden fact at any rate.'

Silence.

'She was pregnant... Six to eight weeks. She miscarried.'

Emer watched the men head off and murmured, 'Now that is what I call an afterthought.'

She recorded some detail in her notebook; time and date of visit, doctor's name, adding to what she'd written last night, for her report, and then made her way to the lift.

She sat by the corporal's bed in a private room. Assessed the sight, which seemed to her to be far worse than the doctor had described. This was a really savage beating.

Emer's blood ran cold with anger. She bit down on her lip for a moment and then said, 'Nora, I know this is extremely difficult for you, but I need to ask you a few questions. Can you hear me?'

Sexton could only half open her 'good' eye.

The faintest of nods.

'Great,' Emer commenced. 'Well, I've spoken to your doctor – there are no lasting injuries, you've heard. So that's hugely positive. My name is Emer and I'm investigating the case. My idea is to have you transferred to UNIFIL Hospital as soon as possible – perhaps by heli. I think it would be better for you there.'

*

Emer glimpsed at a nurse looking in through the window and pushed on. 'Nora, can you remember anything about the night?'

Nora blinked and said almost inaudibly, 'No.'

'The nightclub?'

'No,' said weakly.

'Do you know where Jenny might have gotten to, who she was with?'

No response.

'Nora, who did this to you? Do you know?'

Then a solitary tear.

Mention the miscarriage?

Don't be braindead, Emer. Look at her.

'The Zamba nightclub.'

Emer's prompt came just as the nurse entered, a black woman, who said, 'It is enough for now. She is very agitated.'

Lahr had texted to say he was waiting for her in the hospital café. He pushed a ribbed paper cup of coffee her way and said, 'The police have taken everything. And she had no visitors yesterday, apart from Benny. You, anything?'

'She said she remembered nothing. I couldn't push her. I felt I could have pushed her a little more but a nurse chased me out. We'll get more information from her when she's feeling better – I would hope so.'

'Did you mention the miscarriage?'

'Come on. I thought of it and then thought not to. '

'It might be important intel.'

'Hmm,' she said, thinking it possible her injuries were caused by a falling out between lovers. She might have revealed her news to whoever, and he had turned wounded bear.

'Six to eight weeks,' he said with a nod as though to seal his count was accurate.

Is he really counting his fingers? she thought, issuing him a stony look.

'Two months,' he said, oblivious to her glare. 'This is 12 June. May 12, April 12th. Maybe she got pregnant in Lebanon. What do you think?'

Yes, she thought. But Nora Sexton, Emer suspected, might have arrived in Lebanon in early March, the first week. A while before she had, having come over as part of an advance group. She needed to confirm this, but if her suspicion was spot on, then Nora was almost 15 weeks in Lebanon.

'I need to make a call,' she said.

She rang the UN switchboard and asked to be put through to Sexton's unit orderly room. Emer waited for several minutes, fidgeting with her shirt button, thinking how the case seemed to be forming tributaries. Her gut feeling told her these offshoots ran deep. She sighed after hearing the answer from the Orderly Room Sergeant. 15 weeks.

Emer put another question to him. 'Who is Corporal Sexton's next of kin?'

'So?' Lahr said, after she'd clicked off.

'She arrived in the Leb on the second of March and her husband is her next of kin, David.'

'Is he in Lebanon?'

'No.'

'I see.'

'Yeah. I see too.'

Murky waters, as her father used to say.

CHAPTER 7

That night, Emer could not sleep. She got up and went to the sitting room and reread the touring party statements taken by herself and other military police. They were useless; useless in the sense that there wasn't a scrap of a way forward in any of them. Most ran to about ten sentences and these were riddled with grammatical and spelling errors. The last four statements she saved until last, the soldiers who had disobeyed an order to stay in the hotel to await the investigators' arrival.

She had interviewed the Quartermaster, Hughie Boland, a short, round, balding man with sun-bleached eyebrows, fat fingers with gemstone rings, and chains dangling from his neck. He had to be in his late 40s to early 50s and going through some sort of mid-life crisis. She found it difficult to believe he was in charge of army stores; administratively, applicational, scrupulosity – she could not envisage him ticking all three grades. She would not keep that kind of beast on a short leash. *Bad first impression.* His arrogance, false smile, sunburned round cheeks, the teasing and mock glint coming from his green eyes. *Ach!*

Lahr had recorded the Irish girls' statements: Privates Nicola Lally and Jo Carter.

Each account echoed what the other had said. Talk about a handing around of the hymn sheet. After collating the statements, she understood that everyone on the passenger list would have to be re-interviewed – there were no discrepancies, inaccuracies, nothing stood out that needed verification, except for the fact of there being no discrepancies.

Frustrated at such obvious collusion, she put the papers back in the case file. She hoped Sexton and Casey's statements, when they came on stream, might reveal more. According to Lahr's report, the girls had been nervous and guarded during their interviews.

Definitely holding back. Their body language, their sheer relief when he was done with his questioning, sung from the high heavens. His words reinforced her earlier thoughts: intimidation, self-preservation?

People, she reckoned, had a reason for staying quiet, for distancing themselves from a bad thing that could turn out badly for them.

She picked up her ginger tea and sipped; it was cold. The detachment was shuttered for the night and there wasn't a breath of fresh air: the air conditioning was out of order and the fan on a corner unit toiled without much effect. Emer dipped her eyes in and out of the book she'd been reading, *Where the Jackals Howl* by Israeli writer Amoz Oz, but her eyes grew tired and she was distracted by the case. She got to her feet and turned the light off. She lay on the couch, her head on its armrest. Emer couldn't bring herself to sleep in Chief Joseph's bedroom; it had to do with the portrait of his family, and the sudden experience of loneliness that had come over her like a tall silent wave last night.

She pushed her thoughts to Casey and where she might be, if she was still alive. The longer she remained missing, the more it increased the likelihood of her never being found or being found in a way that no one wanted. No ticking clock but the hands were moving silently.

Emer could not understand the lack of real urgency concerning the probe, that things were being done for the sake of proving at some future date that proper investigative procedure had been followed. Myles O'Rourke telling her that he hadn't reported the soldiers missing because he'd wanted to cut them some slack bothered her. It may well be part of the reason, but she felt he was covering the full picture with half of his hand.

And then Morris jumped into her thoughts, creating a splash; she'd forgotten to brief him.

CHAPTER 8

At first light, she made coffee and went out front. Lit up a small cigar. *Must quit enjoying these.*

The city was stirring to life. Sprinklers came on in a garden across the road. She'd noticed the smooth lawn yesterday, its verges and islands of beautiful irises, tulips, and lilies. A yellow *Egged* bus passed by, clean and modern, unlike the old antiques driven by Arab drivers. A Sherut taxi driver beeped his horn and stopped to pick up two passengers. She thought of the green-domed mosques in Akko, not far from the border, the Crusader church there, where she had stopped off to kill time and had met with a young Irish couple on their honeymoon. They wanted a photograph taken with her – that was nice. That small moment warmed her heart. Drifted her into Dreamworld. They looked so happy.

It rained in the Dominican Republic for hers. Lashed, and the wind tore fronds from palm trees, uprooted traffic signs, ripped corrugated roofs from homes and shops, and the sea had a high lip of foam and a crashing tongue, and they couldn't stay in bed and 'outride it;' as John beerily said. No, they'd to anchor themselves with other hotel guests in a basement until the freak storm sang itself to sleep. Five days of great weather followed. Dust of a memory, her honeymoon, that sometimes left her throat feeling dry. Sad: she and John had married with the fullest intention of living their lives out together. Of course, they were in love. There were moments when the wound of failure had hurt like hell, but time healed, brought her to a coping stage, and after a while she found the memory had lost its potency to cut at her heart.

She stared at her cigar's red eye, inhaled, sipped at her black coffee. She so missed the fresh milk and brown sugar of home –

missed home and its drizzly weather.

'Better ring Morris,' she whispered, and tell him old news that Fredericksen had already heard from Lahr. *How close were those two?* she thought. *Norwegian and Finnish respectively?* It came to her, without any real reason behind her thinking, that she should keep them on her radar – a hunch. *God, do I have a suspicious nature or what? Paranoia?*

An hour later, making their way to the police station to meet with Avi Cohen, the investigating Israeli detective, Hannah, called.

'Hi, Hannah. How are things?'

'Great, and you?'

'Not bad at all. The weather is powerful. Right now, I'm stuck in traffic.'

'Are you home?'

'You're not going to believe this, Hannah. I'm in Jerusalem.'

'Go away out of that. You're kidding. What?'

'My leave was cancelled.'

'Jesus. Has it got to do with the abduction and the assault on the other girl? It's all the news here.'

'Yes.'

'Oh. I see.'

'Listen, Hannah, I really must go.'

'You can't talk, no?'

'Not now. We're just postponing our plans, for a short while, okay? I was so much looking forward to seeing you.'

'Same here. Look, don't worry about it, Emer, you've got your job to do. Just don't forget to buy me some rosary beads from Jerusalem, won't you not? Please. I'll fix you up when you get home.'

'You will not, you're being silly – go on, I'll call later.'

She hung up.

'That was your sister?' Lahr said, moving through traffic lights, eyes taking in road signs, following instructions Benny had given them, a handy route to the police station.

'Yes.'

A one-way street appeared to his left and he indicated and went down it. They came to a barrier and a police sentry let them proceed after first calling Avi Cohen to confirm he was expecting visitors. He gave them directions. After parking in a large courtyard populated with railed-in old cypresses, they got out of the car and stood in the shadow cast by a tree, to determine their bearings. They crossed to an iron stairwell leading to Cohen's office on the second floor.

She'd half expected Avi Cohen to be a fit young man with short black hair, sharp and businesslike. But he was the polar opposite. He looked Indian, was of average height, and had hennaed hair, green-framed spectacles. A cigarette seemed to fall as a natural protrusion from his lips. His smile was forced. The smile of a man who found it difficult to smile.

Names swapped, he said, 'This way,' leaving the small office to enter a larger one.

He sat down behind his desk while indicating for them to sit.

A standing sentinel fan kicked out waves of cool air. Its blades thick with grime. Atop four brown filing cabinets were trays full of documents and behind them bundles of others bound up with twine or thick plastic ties. Air in a water cooler went *plop, plop.*

Cohen said, his accent French slanted, 'Okay. An update. We've released photographs of the missing soldier to the media. We are doing everything as is standard with such a case. The case and the photo will appear on TV, in an Israeli crime awareness show.'

Silence.

'Have you visited the crime scenes?' he asked.

'No,' Lahr said. 'We are going there after this meeting.'

'Hmm. Well, CCTV footage tells us that both soldiers left the hotel together. Sexton was found the next morning, by a camel driver, in the vicinity of the Mount of Olives. She's lucky to be alive; I'm sure you agree. Unfortunately, we don't have much else to go on – my officers are currently taking statements from those we know to have been in the nightclub and are questioning residents in the vicinity. So, I'm still waiting for this information to filter through.'

'Do you need copies of the statements from the UN people?' Lahr said.

'Yes, for my report.'

Emer said, 'What time frame did the incident happen?'

'About 3 a.m., on the 8th. The corporal had consumed quite a lot of alcohol, as reflected in the medical report, and also she'd been using cannabis. We found some roll-ups in her handbag.'

'Her phone?' Emer asked.

'Yes, we have it.'

Lahr said, 'We should have it and her bag.'

'Not yet. It's a continuity of evidence issue, in the event that an Israeli citizen or citizens are responsible for the assault and the kidnapping.'

Emer said, 'What about a print-off of her calls – incoming and outgoing? Just to give us a list of names we can rule in or out of the equation.'

'Okay,' Cohen agreed, running a hand over his hair, 'that should be possible. But her list of names is very short – which suggests that she may have another cell phone.'

'Any voicemail?' Lahr said.

'None.'

'Is it possible to view the security recording?' Emer said, her eyes turned to the TV on a corner shelf.

'Yes, I have it ready.'

He ran the footage. Interior footage, first of the packed club and then of the exit, where the two soldiers could be seen linking each other, approaching a dumpster, passing it by.

'That's it,' Avi said. 'That's what we have of the pair.' He looked from one to the other and added, 'The missing soldier. I think you should prepare for the worst news.'

'Why?'

'There were some dangerous people on that tour bus.'

'We have been told,' Lahr said. 'The Dabrowski brothers.'

'Ah, so you are aware. Tell me then, what can you do about them?'

'Nothing for the moment,' Emer replied.

'Good.'

Good? she thought.

About to ask him why, he glanced at his watch. 'I have to be elsewhere – I'll be back in Jerusalem in a couple of days. Give me a call, then.'

'I...' began Emer.

But he was on the phone, speaking Hebrew. Emer felt as though they'd been suddenly transported to another planet, for Cohen no longer saw them.

She wasn't sure what purpose it served to visit the scenes of crime, as any evidence would surely have been obliterated, but she believed it good practice to fix these scenes in her mind. Mobile phones. She mentioned to Lahr if they should check those belonging to the touring party. He nodded slowly, said he would deal with it. Might be a pointless exercise – as members of the touring party could have more than one phone. Still...

They walked down alleyways leading from the nightclub, took photographs of the nightclub's façade and some interior shots. Then drove to the Mount of Olives, where Sexton had been found.

Darkness fell like a stage curtain as they arrived.

'That's the Church of Ascension over there,' she said, pointing over the rim of her lowered window, 'where Christ left for Heaven – the impression of his footprint is there.'

He said, 'Do you know that there are over 150,000 graves here, with their occupants waiting for the Day of Resurrection to arrive, yes, so they can climb out?'

'I was just about to tell you all about it, Lahr – have we got a torch?'

The Maglite cast a low beam, its battery powering down. They used it at the location where Sexton had been discovered by the camel owner, as pinpointed for them by Cohen. Their look around lasted mere minutes; the battery gave out.

'What are we looking for?' she half whispered to herself more so than to Lahr.

Emer thought, *We're here to say in the report, and if asked at a court of enquiry, that we visited the scene. In reality it serves as much purpose as trying to catch a fart.*

She went on, 'You don't expect to find anything here, do you, seriously? These scenes have been long contaminated by people and—'

'Camel shit!' Lahr said, after stepping in dung.

Muttering complaints, he removed his shoe and wiped its sole against the wall and on a clump of grass.

They moved away from the odour to a low wall and looked westward at the Old City. A crescent moon and stars tattooed the night. She felt the chill of evening raise goosepimples along her forearms.

'I've got no idea why she was brought here,' she said. 'Only Sexton can tell us that. Maybe Casey. Have you got any ideas?'

'None, not yet.'

'If she were left for dead?'

He remained silent.

She went on, teasing out possibilities, 'I think she was dumped here as a warning, or there was a dispute among the kidnappers as to what they should do with her, and she was put here because it was somehow convenient. They wanted her to be found and here was a sure place for that to happen – maybe?'

She paused, waiting.

He wasn't on for talking and that made her curious.

Lahr leaned the flat of his palms on top of the wall. She espied the glint of gold from his wedding band, a widower remaining faithful. And next she thought of a small burst of shooting stars she had witnessed with Hannah, when they were kids and running away from home after Mam had sent them to bed without supper, for being 'bold naughty little f'rs.'

'It's gone cold,' she said, rubbing her upper arms.

'The trail, yes, I'm sure it has,' he said.

'I mean the air has gotten colder.'

'That, also.'

In the car, she wound down the electric window and lit up a cigar, offering him one and asking if he minded her smoking.

'It is too late for you to ask,' he said, smiling.

'I need this. I really do.'

She turned her head and exhaled through the window.

'What now?' he said.

'We search the girls' bedrooms in the hotel and we talk some more to certain people. Benny said he searched Sexton and Casey's room and found nothing of interest there. But it's no harm to cast another eye there. And something else...'

'What?'

'I wonder how many tours the Dabrowski brothers have been on – in fact, how many of the entire party have been on tour during the last few months. It would be interesting to see if the same names appear... wouldn't it? Lahr. For pig iron.'

In the half-light, she saw an abrupt and momentary change to his usual expression: a worried and flinched reaction.

Have I unwittingly said something of significance? she thought.

'What does pig iron mean?' he queried.

Is that what she had seen, puzzlement, and not a flinch depicting concern?

'It means for the hell of it, just being curious,' she replied.

He nodded.

'It was something O'Rourke said, about other soldiers going missing on previous tours. Benders, he said. But maybe for business, too. What do you think?'

'Are you going to smoke all of that?' he said, not smiling.

'One more pull.'

And after inhaling and breathing out a dense blue-grey cloud, she flicked the cigar out the window and watched its arc and fall.

'Hotel,' she said.

CHAPTER 9

Emer watched Myles O'Rourke's body language as he walked across the foyer towards her. Gone was the confident expert on Middle East culture; his shoulders were hunched and his eyes were like lost eagles caught out in a storm, not knowing where to roost.

He said, 'I've instructed them to wait in their rooms for you and your team and to cooperate fully.' A frown knitted his brow as he went on, 'I don't understand why you're doing this. What are you looking for, exactly?'

'Anything and everything,' Emer replied. 'I mean, we found nothing in the statements we took from your people, nothing that might help us to find Casey or those who almost beat the life out of Sexton. So, we have to use our imagination.'

'Hmm,' he said, ordering a coffee from the bartender.

'A question for you,' she said.

He gave her a sidelong look. 'I wish you'd run out of those.'

'A dose of the truth usually kills them off.'

'What's your question?' he said wearily.

'You've got no idea who distributed the handout, have you?'

'Handout? You've lost me.'

'You see, nearly all of the statements given to us – they read much the same.'

'I can't help you there. I don't own their tongues, do I?'

He thrust at her a list of rooms and their occupants. Their eyes locked briefly. *You should never corner a rat*, she thought. Turning from him, she beckoned Benny Rafal and gave him the list.

'Benny, get the keys of the tour bus from Dabrowski and have Pedney search it also.'

Minutes later, outside Room 145, on the third floor, Emer rapped twice on the door. Moments later, a young soldier with a blaze of acne across her forehead let her in.

Emer stepped inside, closed the door and leaned her back against it. She studied the two soldiers sitting on the edge of the double bed.

The soldiers were dressed in civvies.

'You are?' Emer said quietly to the soldier who'd opened the door.

'I'm Carter, she's Lally.'

Carter was ashen-faced, unwashed hair and sunken eyes, while Nicola Lally was hard-faced and sullen, like she'd swallowed something she was trying to keep down. In Lally, Emer recognised signs of disapproval and resentment. She had a problem with authority; strange that trait hadn't been picked up on during recruit training. Lally removed her T-shirt, displaying her breasts, and put on a white T-shirt and pulled up a pair of tracksuit bottoms. Her eyes held mild contempt. Daring eyes.

Glancing around the room, Emer saw pizza cartons, empty beer and spirit bottles, an ashtray with ends of roll-ups. Clothes lay in bundles on the fawn carpet. A hillock of bras, knickers, and T-shirts.

'Hmm,' Emer said. 'I bet if I were to really tear this room apart, that I would find hash, prescription pills – in fact, I probably wouldn't have too much ripping apart to bring illegal stuff to light; stuff that would bring serious questions for you girls to answer. I'm quite certain that no matter how well you think you've disposed of them, I would find something. Some little thing, *girls.*'

Jo Carter stared between her knees at the faded scarlet rug. Nicola Lally's face betrayed no emotion.

'Extend your hands in front of you,' Emer said. 'Good. Now turn them over.'

Clear of cuts and abrasions. Neither had long fingernails. That's something. At least they weren't the kind whose manners seldom match the gloss on their talons.

'Excellent, a positive start. No signs of either of you having been involved in a catfight with Corporal Sexton.'

Lally sat on a chair by the window. She opened it halfway, allowing in the noise of passing traffic, but also a welcome breeze. A curtain stirred. Carter remained on the edge of the bed, seemingly welded there.

Emer said, 'Your statements told me nothing and I don't believe either of you when you say that you know nothing about what went down.'

No response. Carter crossed her ankles, examined a pimple on her elbow as though it were a new arrival.

Emer crossed the floor and opened the wardrobe. She peered inside, ran her gloved right hand over the top shelf and brought a chair to stand on to look at the top. Dust. Next, she looked under the bed, pulled out the drawers of bedside lockers and dresser.

Silence. Punctuated by the sound of car and truck horns.

She picked up the butt of a roll-up from the ashtray and sprinkled flakes into a miniature plastic drug-testing bag. Showed it to them seconds later, after the fluid changed colour.

'You're in trouble, girls.'

Silence.

'Really, neither of you has a scrap of information to help with the investigation into the serious assault on a comrade soldier – and we have another missing in action. Do I have to set out a questionnaire to corner you? Or push this bullshit drug rap on you both?'

Emer sighed.

'Really,' she repeated, thinking that perhaps whatever chance she had of making inroads with Carter, she'd little or none with Lally.

'Tell me this, what is Corporal Sexton like?' she asked, deciding to keep the pair together for now. 'Private Carter? You start – look at me.'

Carter shrugged, would not look directly at Emer, then tried to but couldn't hold the gaze.

'She was okay,' she said. 'I wouldn't, like, know her all that well.'

'But this is your third time across the border with her in the last six weeks.'

The Transport NCO back at HQ had compiled the records and texted the info to Emer en route to the hotel.

'And your third time too, Nicola – you both must love the Holy Land very much.'

'The fun part, yeah, for sure,' Lally said. 'Anywhere is better than Lebanon. It's a right dive.'

'Nora Sexton, Corporal Lally, did you get along with her?'

'She was all right, but she liked to talk – she never shut up talking,' Lally said, 'and she was like you – she'd get in your face about stuff.'

'Private Carter?' Emer pressed, choosing to ignore Lally's comment.

'She never gave me any hassle.'

'Did she hassle anyone?'

Carter shrugged.

'What about Jenny?' Emer asked.

'She was sound,' Lally said.

Although aware that Nicola Lally had already spoken of Sexton in the past tense, she thought it a habit, but decided to confirm. 'You said was?'

'Is, I mean.'

'Did either of you know that Nora was pregnant?'

Silence.

'I mean was, not is,' Emer said.

For the first time since she had entered the room, the two privates looked at each other with puzzled expressions.

'Here's the deal,' Emer said. 'You give me the name of the man she was sleeping with and I'll walk from here – there'll be no arrests, no handcuffs, no red asterisks on record.'

'Nicola?' Carter said.

Lally's lips turned down in disgust at Jo's giveaway response.

Carter said nervously, 'It was the Polish driver. Maybe. Because she was also seeing Quartermaster Hughie Boland. So…'

Emer waited for something else to fall, but nothing grew in the quietness.

Finally, she said, 'Is there anything that either of you would like to add?'

When no answer was forthcoming, Emer said, 'Wait outside, Private Lally.'

She did not want to leave Carter alone with Emer and hesitated.

'Don't worry… you'll get your turn to talk,' Emer said.

With her room share gone, Jo Carter appeared to seize up in terror. Her shoulders climbed and her hands shook a little.

She said, 'Ma'am, I've got nothing more to say – you can do me for the drugs, I don't care.'

'Who are you afraid of?'

'No one. I've got nothing to say.'

'Get off the bed.'

Hesitantly, Carter rose.

'Lift the mattress.'

A spread of glossy magazines lay on the base. Not a stash of drugs, as she'd presumed.

Emer said, 'Hold the mattress for me,' as she reached for them.

Recent issues, she thought. *Five, six.*

Carter eased the mattress down as Emer leafed through the magazines.

'Are these yours?' she said.

Specialist magazine: antiques, marketplaces, buy and sell, advertisements, articles about recent finds. The latest issue was a week old.

'No, they're not mine.'

'Whose?'

'I don't know.'

Carter sat down on the edge of the bed, folded her arms across her chest.

'Who put them under the mattress?'

'It wasn't me.'

'Who?'

A shrug.

'Someone did, Carter. People don't usually stash this type of magazine under a bed, do they? It's not exactly Penthouse for Ladies.'

Emer waited.

'What's going on here? Carter? Come on.'

'Nothing, I haven't got a clue how the books ended up there, or who owns them, or anything else.'

'So your fingerprints won't show up on them?'

'Will you send in Private Lally?'

Her head was downcast. So, Lally was responsible. Carter had said so, without saying it directly.

'Yes, send her in.'

Private Lally, upon entering, noticed the magazines. She slouched against the wall, under a painting of ruins and camels resting beside a village well.

'I found these under the mattress,' Emer said.

'So?'

'Stand up straight, soldier – what is your problem?'

'I haven't got one.'

'If I have fingerprints lifted from these magazines, will I find yours on them?'

'Fingerprints, are you serious? OTT, if you ask me.'

'It wouldn't be done perhaps for a minor investigation, but for a violent assault and kidnapping, yeah, for sure. Don't you understand the seriousness of this?'

'I put the magazines there.'

'Why?'

'I was minding them for the captain.'

'Myles O'Rourke.'

'Yes.'

'He told you to hide them?'

'No, not hide, just to keep them safe for him. He said they'd walk if he left them in his room. Everyone wanted to read them, but no one wanted to buy them, that sort of thing.'

'And they ended up under the mattress because you had guests coming in and out?' Emer said gently.

'Yes, well, we all went in and out of each other's rooms, those we're friends with, it was no big deal.'

'Who would have come in here?'

'Hughie, Janus, Lukas, Myles, mainly.'

Emer matched the names: Hughie the mid-life crisis man, Janus the guy who'd scared Benny, his brother, the driver Lukas, and Myles, Mister Coin Man… Quite the quartet.

'You can go. Both of you wait outside the room until I've finished my search. Leave the door open, so you can look in. I couldn't have you accusing me of planting stuff, could I?'

She searched the room thoroughly and then left with the magazines. Lally's eyes were on them, probably asking herself if she should challenge Emer's right to confiscate them.

In the foyer, Lahr and the others were waiting for her. The room searches hadn't revealed anything noteworthy. The search of the bus had turned up almost nothing of interest, save for a blue-glazed figurine of a demon, its size the length and width of her hand. Its tongue peeped from the centre of its mouth, in an expression of pure, grotesque rage. Three lines of cuneiform were inscribed deeply along its back. A solid plinth held intricately done inlaid images of snakes and other markings she thought similarly patterned to ancient Celtic script.

Lahr said, 'Pedney got into the luggage compartment and found this hidden under some oily rags. Benny is in shock because he had already searched inside and found nothing.'

Odd, Emer thought, that Benny Rafal would have failed to find the object. He had the appearance of a man whose eyes would not miss too much. Perhaps he did not look too hard, believing there was nothing to find?

'Isn't it an ugly-looking thing?' she said, weighing it on the palm of her hand. 'And heavy, too.'

Emer eased the idol into an evidence bag Lahr held open.

'What are you thinking?' Lahr quizzed.

'At worst it's someone's lost item, at best it might be telling us something,' she replied, gently pushing a couple of the magazines to his chest. 'In light of Pedney's discovery, maybe we should read through these.'

'I just love this type of magazine,' he said, skimming the titles, 'and eh, we're needed back in HQ tomorrow – Fredericksen wants a meeting.'

She thought to say something but just sighed. Israel is where the crime scene is at, not Lebanon.

'I know,' he agreed, putting the magazines into his satchel. 'I suggested one of us should stay behind. But…'

'Do you know what I think, Lahr?' she said. 'Maybe we should perhaps cross the border this very evening – the touring party, the whole shebang. Why wait for tomorrow?'

His lips practically disappeared and the corners of his mouth turned down. She was taken aback at how the suggestion had wrought such prominent signs of stress.

'I…' he began. 'Is there a reason why it can't wait?'

'Is there a reason why it should? The touring party hasn't displayed an ounce of empathy and concern for Casey's plight and Sexton's condition – are they helping us any? No, in fact they're displaying a very hostile and unhelpful attitude – is that not sticking in your throat? Are there no alarm bells ringing in your head?'

Lahr blocked his eyes with his hand and then brought it to his side. His smile was fake and polite as he said, 'Anything else?'

'We should search the bus again before we make tracks for the border.'

'You're right,' Lahr conceded. 'Their leave period is over anyway.'

Why the resistance? Has he made plans or something? A date? No. The blue idol, wouldn't he be anxious to see what that's about? And get it across the border? The magazines are telling us something, for sure.

She took a deep breath and told herself to chill. She was not in command. Fredericksen had made that abundantly clear. Yet she felt as though she was in charge; that somehow she'd slid naturally into the position. Lahr had something of a reticence about him, a softly-softly does it, as though he feared stepping on toes.

Or is that my imagination?

And what about Rafal – if he had come across the idol, would he have told us?

Look at him. He has the head of an angry man whose numbers came up in the Lotto, on the one occasion he hadn't bought them.

Someone touched her head gently and she turned, but there was no one behind her.

Someone had definitely caressed her hair.

Lahr said, 'Are you okay?'

'Yes, I'm fine,' she said.

'Okay,' he said, 'we'll leave for the border within the hour.'

He wore his wedding band. It glared sunshine. Hers had been thrown into the Liffey in anger, but not her engagement ring, not even in vestigial temper – this she had pawned for less than half its worth. She'd studied the rings in the window of Flannery's Antiques, debating whether she should flog hers – prices varied from e4,000 to e9,700. Thought of the fingers they'd once adorned, strings of bones now. Chasing the wind, chasing money, chasing this and that, despite knowing we can never hold on to it. Nothing is ever *caught.*

CHAPTER 10

The next morning, back in her billet at UN Headquarters in south Lebanon, Emer was woken by the noise of a helicopter taking off. It was just past 7. She got up and went to the minifridge. Her mouth was dry from last night's merlot and two cigars. She and Lahr took time out last night in Pablo's Inn, dined on mushroom risotto and French fries. He had been good company, quiet, with a dry and droll sense of humour. Her type of company. She saw he was burdened. He missed his late wife and his daughter. He didn't say so, but the mention of home, the absence brought a shine to his eyes. Then a joke from either, a lessening of the intensity, put them back onto a more convivial subject.

She raised the hem of the mosquito net canopying her bed and slid out, her feet feeling for and then easing into toeless sandals. Emer turned on the radio but kept the volume low.

Dressed in a clean, light green uniform, she ran a couple of baby wipes over her face and sprayed deodorant underarm. Fredericksen, Lahr, and Myles O'Rourke the coin advisor would be in attendance. Morris, too. He had called her yesterday to say that he would have a private chat with her prior to the MP meeting.

She hurried past the French Post Office: UNBPO, United Nations Base Post Office. It was a faster postal system than the Irish had at their disposal and some of the Irish contingent preferred to use it. She was an emailer and a phone caller, but for a kid's birthday, you needed to send a surprise parcel.

Lahr spotted her from the steps leading into Fredericksen's office and waved at her to hurry. She was the last to arrive in the room. Breathless. Morris glared at her; no time for their private conversation.

Fredericksen's desk was fronted by five chairs in an arc.

Morris told O'Rourke to wait outside. Judging by his sheepish look, Emer suspected a Morris broadside was still smarting the man's ears.

'Okay, Lahr,' Fredericksen said, 'you can begin.'

Emer knew what he was going to say and felt her attention waning as he moved along. *God, I could have done with another hour in bed, and a decent fry-up.*

After Lahr finished, Morris addressed Emer. 'The room searches yielded no clues at all? So why did you think they were necessary – did you think Casey was hiding?'

Emer pursed her lips, as though to cork a sharp rebuke. He wasn't police. She looked to Lahr and Fredericksen, thinking it was their place to point this out. Stupid question.

She said, 'A flippant question, sir. You're dead wrong. We found Casey's passport and there were 800 dollars in her kit bag and 200 euros... so these clues tell us she had no plans to desert. Her bank account back home has had no withdrawals since her disappearance.'

F you, she thought.

'And you call those clues?' Morris said with mild disdain.

'Well, what would you refer to them as, sir. Bedbugs?'

Lahr interjected, 'Carry on, Emer.'

'Right now, the Israeli police are conducting a search for Private Casey. Unlike a search for a missing person back home, when friends and family members and community join in, this won't happen here. Her tour buddies, by the way, don't seem overly concerned about their comrades – if they do, they haven't revealed that concern. That, too, Colonel Morris, is a clue. Or a pointer, if that suits your palate.'

Pushing it – would you look at his puss? Like his 24-carat shit has backed up his throat.

Fredericksen spread his hands flat on the desk. 'Lahr, this statue that you found and the magazines… you have these in an SIS safe?'

'The idol, yes. We are reading the magazines.'

'In the office, not in your billets,' warned Fredericksen. 'They could become a crucial evidential link in the case. You might have to demonstrate the continuity of evidence, the trail of where they have been, if the evidence has been in any way compromised. But you know this.'

Fredericksen raised an eyebrow at Morris who took the cue and said, 'A number of people on that tour bus have regularly been to Israel in the last three months: Boland, Sexton, Carter, Lally, Casey, the Dabrowski brothers and O'Rourke. It's probably a bit excessive.'

Emer nodded. *Tell me something new*, she thought.

Morris went on, 'The figurine – we think it would be a good idea to have it appraised. It might be worth zilch. As we Irish say of futility: *'Tis hard to drive a hare out of a bush he's not in.* Suspicions of a smuggling ring in operation might be groundless.'

Fredericksen took over. 'I've already organised for someone to examine the artefact. She's coming from the American university in Beirut. I sent her a picture of it, which is why she's hurrying to see it in person.'

He's on the ball. Great.

'Lieutenant Lahr?' Fredericksen said. 'If there's anything you need, let me know.'

'Sir.'

'Captain Harte, do you have anything to add?'

'I think the primary case is developing other strands, and the discovery of the idol is an alarming turn. So, my hunch – and it's only that for now – is that both the assault and the missing soldier case are interlinked with its discovery. And as already mentioned by Captain Lahr, when you factor in the presence of the Polish Mafia…'

The fall into silence was loud. She could hear the sound of the sea 100 metres to her right, behind the club.

'The cell phones?' she said, looking to Lahr.

'Nothing of interest – and no resistance from anyone to surrendering their phones. They have others, I expect.'

Fredericksen indicated to Morris that he should speak.

'Meantime, Captain Harte,' Morris said as he studied Emer, 'you're going to be on TV to discuss Private Casey with RTE Television – they've sent a news team over. I'll discuss it with you after the meeting – what to say and what not. As you can imagine, this is huge news back home.'

TV, she thought.

Me?

The last time she'd appeared on TV was nine years ago after she'd reached the final of a national Irish boxing championship, which she'd lost by a split decision to a remarkable younger talent. Emer remembered her opponent as being lithe and tough, and a difficult target to pin down. *Story of my life.*

'Is that okay with you, sir?' she said, looking at Fredericksen then Lahr. *Obviously, it is*, she thought, *but surely Lahr as the officer leading the case should be the one to speak?* Resentment at the double check of his authority made Morris grimace. His look would have wilted a flower.

This interview was full on in her face, with questions picking at the progress of the investigation – what had and hadn't been done and what was yet to happen. She couldn't give the reporters any facts, nothing more than a sketchy outline. Even if she possessed information, well, feeding it to the media wouldn't be good police work, unless it was done with the intention to advance the standing of the investigation.

Just as she thought the interview was being wound up, the interviewer's expression and tone changed.

'Captain Harte, are we to believe reports of a smuggling ring involving UN soldiers?'

Oh, Jesus... Where did she hear that?

Emer smiled and said, 'If you've got information relating to that, UNIFIL Military Police would love to hear more from you.'

'It's common talk on the street outside the camp.'

'I haven't heard of it – I'm deep into finding the missing Irish soldier and in determining what exactly happened to Corporal Sexton, so if you excuse me...'

'Is it true that Irish soldiers might be involved in—'

Emer brushed past the woman and the cameraman, saying, 'Please, I have a job to do.'

'You came across well on the screen,' Morris later said, in the Irish Officers' Mess on the hill near the administration block. 'Well done... Now, now – and I've cleared this with Fredericksen. You're going to stay in Israel to push this search for Casey. I've booked you a hotel room in Netanya and you will have the use of an MP saloon. You can claim expenses but keep receipts. I'm a man who doesn't like to stumble across tripwires. In other words, leave me a paper trail.'

'Yes, sir. I can do that much, search. But I haven't got a clue where to next...'

'You had better find a roadmap, then. At the end of the day there's going to be an inquiry, probably more than one, and I want to be able to prove that we did our utmost to find Private Casey.'

'Lahr?'

'He'll mop up things here and then he'll be available to assist you. And you have the MP detachment in Jerusalem to call upon, and also the MPs in Nahariya, too.'

'I've got a few interviews to conduct.'

I'm going to poke a hornets' nest, to see what moves.

'Well, try to be on the road by tomorrow afternoon, at the latest.'

'Sir,' she said, thinking his tone more respectable toward her.

'And Harte?'

'Sir?'

'You're right, a clue is a pointer.'

She had read somewhere that in war, yesterday is a long time ago and tomorrow isn't beyond your nose, and the worst of atrocities are perpetrated when soldiers suspect there's literally not a tomorrow for them... Morals are put aside, replaced by a prevailing sense of imminent doom. Rape, murder... looting... smuggling...

CHAPTER 11

Emer called in a Polish translator and drove to the Polish Logistics Company to interview the Dabrowski brothers. Lahr had been summoned to report to the Finnish Battalion HQ in the mountains, so he said. He'd qualified for his UN Service Medal and was required to participate in the medal parade.

There was an MP detachment close to the Finnish camp, across the border, in northern Israel, Metula. Dudevant Street, she recalled. Horrid little ground-floor apartment. He hadn't mentioned the medal parade to her the other night, and these parades weren't planned at the last minute. He'd forgotten? Perhaps there was a visiting dignitary he wanted to speak with in connection to his daughter's health, to lobby him into funding a new treatment that wasn't in the health system. Or perhaps he simply wanted time out.

She sat in an office procured for her by a heavyset Polish officer. A small, musty room cluttered with filing cabinets and an accumulation of broken office furniture. Preferring to face the interviewee with no barrier between them, she moved the desk aside. If her suspicions were well founded, she wasn't going to be told a whole ton, but this way she'd get to see more body language: finger knitting, knee quaking, fidgeting, heel going like a piston, and more...

First up, Janus Dabrowski, the driver's older brother. Mafia. The man who had scared Benny Rafal.

He was nothing like his brother; tall, broad-chested with finely sculpted cheekbones. He wore a Rolex watch and spiral leather wristbands on his other arm. A gold cross hung from a large, linked chain.

'Sit,' she said quietly.

Emer crossed her legs, blue clipboard on her lap. She kept one hand underneath it.

She asked him for his UN ID card and he opened his camouflage-patterned wallet and handed it to her. Emer noted his long fingers, the thick gold wedding band, the bitten fingernails. After recording his details at the top of the statement she handed him his card.

'How may I help you?' he said, eyes narrowed.

The interpreter stepped away from Emer, as though to show Dabrowski he was not here of his own volition.

'In many ways,' she said. 'What do you know of the Irish soldier who was brutally assaulted and the other who is missing?'

'Nothing.' He shrugged.

'Nothing.'

'That is exactly what I said.'

'You must like the Holy Land, to visit it so many times?'

'I love it.' He brought his forefinger to his cross.

He stared at her, rested his hands flat on his thighs, parted his knees slightly and raised his heels from the scruffy brown lino. He smirked as he gently rocked the chair a couple of times, before stopping.

'You can go,' she said, gesturing dismissively, knowing this would draw a reaction.

He glanced at the interpreter and then brought his hard almond eyes to her.

'Do you know who I am?' he said.

'Not really, but I know what you are.'

He drew phlegm to his mouth and spat to the side, then confronted her: his face inches from hers. Though shaken a little by his abrupt shift to aggression, she remained calm.

He said with scarcely concealed spite, 'Your sister is very pretty, I think. Hannah. She has such a lovely and beautiful ass. At least we think so, my Irish friends and I.'

The interpreter said something in Polish. A pleading for him not to hurt her, she suspected. Dabrowski barked at him and he scurried from the room, closing it behind him, gently. She guessed he'd been told to do that and to wait outside.

Suddenly Dabrowski's mouth went into a wide O, as though he'd been doused with ice-cold water.

'Oh, you feel it. Good. And yes, it is loaded and cocked against your genitalia,' Emer said firmly. 'It's your call, but you are one head-to-toe prick, so maybe you could survive life without your tiny maggot. My Polish girlfriends tell me it's huge in one way, as in a disappointment. Now bring your puss and bad breath away.'

He brought his head back. 'The world is a small place, you should know. There are many Poles working in Ireland.'

'Is that a threat?'

'Are you recording this?'

'What? My holding a gun to you? Don't be stupid.'

'I'm far from that.'

'Your looks are deceiving.'

He glared at her.

She said, 'Get up and get out and send that coward in.'

He stood, kicked back the chair, and gave her a long threatening look, before leaving.

The interpreter ventured in, not expecting to see her in one piece.

'Next,' she said, over a cough.

She hauled in two quick deep breaths to compose herself.

Janus's brother, Lukas, a blob of a man, declined to furnish her with a statement, saying he had already given the military police one at the hotel. He sweated profusely and dabbed a tissue to his forehead several times.

'I have nothing more to say,' he said in Polish.

The interpreter relayed this to her. She nodded. Emer believed Dabrowski knew enough English to engage with her but chose not to, so as to frustrate and hinder her line of questioning.

'Ask him if he knew Corporal Sexton was pregnant.'

The interpreter baulked.

'Ask.'

Dabrowski clenched his fists. His cheeks crimsoned. She smelled the salty reek of his anger. His eyes tried to burn her.

'Tell him I could be wrong – maybe Hughie Boland is the father. I'm sure Sexton's husband is going to be asking questions, don't you think?'

Again, the interpreter baulked.

'Tell him.'

Dabrowski shot to his feet. Towered over her. If his brother had warned him about what was under her clipboard, he didn't seem to care.

'Ask him why he is upset, would you?'

The interpreter spoke.

Dabrowski's response sounded guttural.

'He said to tell you that he is more than upset.'

She wrote in his statement. 'Tell him, I'm writing that he is not happy.'

Silence.

'He can go now. And you, too, for a few minutes. I'll call you back in.'

Her business here was done. She'd ventured into the pit, and had matters confirmed. UN soldiers had turned on their own, beaten one and caused another to vanish. There was so much menace in both men, so much cutting steel – the question now, was why? What was their motivation? *Greed, Emer... Wakie, wakie.*

Hannah? Information probably gleaned from his Irish friends. It wouldn't have been a major task to find out. Obviously, these men had had much previous success with their intimidation tactics; they knew how to persuade people to back off. If someone had enough courage to stand up to them, they took aim at the person's family.

Many criminals used this sort of threat against family members but for most, it remained a threat they never followed through. It could easily bounce back against their own. Revenge was a boomerang. There was always a chance, though, of a threat morphing into a reality.

Suddenly, she recalled speaking with Hannah on the phone with Benny Rafal and Lahr and Lahr asking her about Hannah being her sister. No... no – she was being paranoid.

Emer got to her feet and rested the pistol on top of the nearest filing cabinet. Her knees buckled, quivered, and she clasped her hands to the edge of the desk. She wanted to vomit. Retched. Her stomach seemed as though it wanted to violently eject something. Ice-cold anxiety burst across the nape of her neck, and down the length of her spine. She shivered. She hurried to light a cigar but gave up trying because of her shakiness. She held her hands out in front of her. Her fingers shook, each one...

CHAPTER 12

By late afternoon, she felt composed enough to resume interviewing and drove to Transport Headquarters. This time, she did not bring her service pistol and kept the desk between her and Hughie Boland, Quartermaster. Mr Mid-life Crisis himself. Instinct told her he was on the Dabrowskis' payroll, and while a dangerous man, not quite so much as the Poles.

Sure he would give *another* statement, he said cheerfully. And went on to yield almost verbatim the same statement. Exasperating. She was uncertain about asking him if anyone on the tour party had lost anything.

The earlier interviews had strung her out a little, and her mind was distracted, unsure of what she should do about the veiled threats to Hannah. She decided to risk the enquiry.

Momentarily, the sun slipped from his face.

'Such as?' he said.

'A little money and some personal property.'

'I haven't heard of anyone losing anything and as for money,' Boland said, the smile returning, 'it wouldn't be like any of those misers to lose so much as a shekel. What money they lost wouldn't be enough to blind a midge.'

His smile returned in full – a phoney canvas.

Well, he'd heard something or knew something, she realised, because it had been etched on his face, as black and loud as a newspaper banner. The blue-gazed artefact.

'Oh, one more thing,' she said, about to deliver a question that had brought a cutting glare and murderous intention from Lukas

Dabrowski. 'Did you know that Nora Sexton was pregnant?'

A frown etched along his forehead. 'How the hell would I know that?'

'So you'd have no objection to providing a DNA sample?'

Well now, isn't that a pure mask of contempt?

'That is a serious allegation, ma'am. I'll have you know that I am a very happily married man.'

'It isn't an allegation. Of course it isn't. You would be dismissing yourself from our considerations, in that way saving us time and effort. Cooperation... You've heard of the word?'

'Piss off.'

'Temper, temper...'

'Catch you later,' she said cheerfully, getting up to leave the room.

'You will,' he spat, so venomously it stalled her at the door.

She looked him up and down in mute contempt and left.

None of the men had asked her about Sexton's condition, or if there'd been any new development concerning Casey. Such blatant disregard irked the hell out of her.

Mentally and physically tired and frayed, she was almost relieved to hear the doctor advising her against interviewing Sexton for at least another week. The battered corporal wasn't emotionally or mentally ready to receive visitors, let alone an MP.

'She doesn't want to speak with you,' he said, bluntly.

CHAPTER 13

Emer brought a chair from her billet and sat outside to watch the sun's glowing descent into the sea.

Lebanon. Tomorrow, Israel. She sipped from a glass of whiskey and smoked a cigarillo. A book squatted on her thigh, one she'd borrowed from the library, and well beyond its return date. *The Devil's Advocate* by Morris West. Hannah recommended it, about a priest sent by the Vatican to investigate another priest, who was living with a woman, or at least that was the gist of the story.

She couldn't concentrate. Every few seconds her mind wandered to the investigation; something she might do or say or shouldn't have said or done. She was deep in it now; she compared the entanglement to being in a dense wood at night and getting caught up in bramble while searching for a way out.

She worried a little for her own personal safety but more so for Hannah's. Emer was a soldier; before that, a policewoman; every facet of her life seemed to have an element of danger attached. Boxing, rock climbing... bloody marriage, she thought, the whiskey kicking in. Music played from a CD player, the Furies with the *Red Rose Café*... One of Mam's favourites.

Emer detested life's prickly reminders of those passed on, their cropping up unannounced, as they induced sadness and brought her to tears. Such as now. She let them fall unfettered.

In the morning, after breakfast, she strolled down the hill to the MP camp, wearing shades. She could spend forever in a country like this, where the sun was no stranger, where you could plan a day's excursion confident it wouldn't rain. Other times, she wished for rain.

Stepping into the MP Investigation Office, she was greeted by Fredericksen and the antiquities expert from Beirut. No sign of Lahr, who'd told her he'd be back after his medal ceremony, to see her before she departed for Israel.

Fredricksen introduced her to Marcella Thomas from the American university in Beirut. Marcella, Emer thought, resembled the pale actress from the movie *Gorillas in the Mist*. She wore a long blue blouse that fell over white crinkled slacks. She was pale faced, with dark circles under her eyes. Indications she'd heard someone say of hashish use or a bad heart.

Emer got the key from a drawer in Lahr's desk and unlocked the safe, then twisted the code on the dial. She reached in and surfaced the evidence bag, brought it to the desk, and broke the seal, taking note of the time and date.

'Oh, sweet Lord!' Marcella stated, her eyes widened with astonishment.

She patted the idol, ran her fingertips up and down the blue glaze, traced them along its inscription and picked it up.

Emer watched her slowly place the object down before consulting a thick hardbound book. Marcella pointed to the glossy close-up of photographs on a double spread. Three idols encased in glass, seated on a shelf, listed underneath as being part of an inventory of looted stock.

'I'm in complete awe,' she said. 'Might I ask where exactly you found this piece?'

'We can't say. Not yet,' Fredericksen replied. He scratched at his eyebrow and declared, 'I was hoping to hear you determine it was junk and worth a little more than nothing.'

'No. This is a very rare piece,' she said, bringing a magnifying glass to the figurine. 'Are there others? There are six of these in total – they make up a set that's known as the Six Demons of Ur; the God Marduk's prodigies.'

'This is the only one that's come into our possession,' Emer said. The thing gave her the creeps; she even refrained from looking at its yellow gemstone eyes. It was as though they could see and were looking right back at her.

'They were looted from a museum in Baghdad during the 2003 American blitz of the Iraqi capital,' Marcella said. 'There's a huge underworld market for such rarities. It's so goddamn awful how people destroy their heritage – the Iraqi authorities will want it back, for sure. I know a couple of their museum personnel quite well, so if you would like…'

'They're welcome to it,' Fredericksen said. 'I'll speak directly with the UN Force Commander and speed things along – while you might notify your associates.'

Marcella nodded, staring at the idol.

Emer asked, 'What's its value?'

'Oh, about 250, even 300,000 US dollars, that would be a conservative estimate – but if someone wanted it for ritual purposes, to complete ownership of all six, why… Maybe the seller could push for 500,000.'

'My. What sort of rituals?' Emer asked.

'Perhaps human and animal sacrifice,' Marcella said, putting the tip of her forefinger into an inlaid character. 'I have no idea what the script means, and I know how to translate cuneiform – it probably won't make sense unless read in conjunction with the other idols. But… Wow! This is really such an amazing find. Can I take some photographs? I'd love to email my Iraqi friends about its discovery right away.'

How anyone could gush lovingly over such a monstrosity escaped Emer, especially when fully aware of its past and for what it was used.

CHAPTER 14

Lahr invited her to lunch at Pablo's Inn on the shanty street directly outside the UN compound. He had arrived just as Fredericksen and Marcella Thomas were making their way to the International Dining Complex. Emer didn't like the food there; it was bland and badly cooked. She'd heard a story of a French cook putting a dead rat through the mincer. Could be an urban legend, but some soldiers were capable of doing anything to alleviate boredom.

Pablo served them. They sat indoors because passing traffic kicked up dust and spat out noise. Two pizzas and two beers. Music played quietly in the background. Large turtle shells were fastened to the walls and a fishing net sagged from the ceiling.

'Where is Morris putting you up?' Lahr asked.

'Hotel Samuel in Netanya. It's got half a star rating.'

A smile cut across his face, like a slice of moon appearing from behind a smoky cloud. He had been pretty sullen till then. Something niggled at him. Or maybe he had a medal parade hangover and his head was thumping.

'Just to bring you up to speed,' she said, 'I interviewed the Dabrowski brothers yesterday and Hughie Boland.'

He nodded absentmindedly, his hand under his chin. Her news seemed not to be 'news' to his ears.

The beers arrived and they clinked bottles, said cheers. Emer waited for him to ask how she'd gotten on.

He slugged at his beer. She noticed an old scar on his forearm, a white strip in otherwise tanned and lightly fair-haired skin and wondered how he came by it.

'They are dangerous men,' she said. 'I can confirm that.'

Resented having to tell him this, instead believing he should have been peppering her with questions.

'You didn't need to have it confirmed, did you?' he said, tilting his bottle at her. 'You knew it, Emer. Benny told us. Yes, of course, they are involved in Casey's disappearance and Sexton's assault – so why did you antagonise them?'

'I thought they needed to have their cages rattled, because do you know what, Lahr? I'm pretty pissed off about the hiding Sexton got. And as for Casey, my heart is breaking for her and her family, because those bastards most likely raped her and then wasted her. So, that's why… And…'

Silence.

She brushed pizza crumbs off her chest. His eyes lighted on her boobs, almost as solid as a touch.

She smiled at his blushes after he realised that she'd noticed.

He coughed and indicated she go on.

'I feel we're tiptoeing around these arseholes, and as for you, Lahr, what the hell are you playing at, disappearing yesterday and for most of the morning? You might be in charge but I have the impression that you're standing back and letting me do pretty much most of the donkey work.'

Another round of thickly cut French fries and two beers arrived.

'It's an Irish case,' he said almost laconically, 'so, I'm the overseer. Is that the right word?'

She held her gaze on Pablo's back until he was behind the bar and couldn't overhear.

'You're killing my appetite,' she said. 'It's a bloody case with several nationalities involved, and the discovery of the idol has given it another dimension – smuggling – are you acting the thick, and if so, why?'

'I've handled major cases like this in Finland. You're feeling out of your depth because of your lack of experience, that's all, but you're doing very well, covering most of the angles. I'm impressed.'

'Don't patronise.'

'I'm not. I think perhaps you should stand back a little, though. Be like me. You will see and learn more from a distance.'

He sliced his pizza in half, dipped a chip in ketchup.

'You mean... sleepwalk?'

'I mean,' he said, waving the chip, 'for you to remember that you are passing through Lebanon and Israel – this time next year you will be home. If you step back, you will see the play unfold.'

'I don't follow.'

'These men are dangerous; you have established this,' he said, eating his chip.

She studied him for a few moments, not knowing what to say, trying to read the huge landfill of shit he wasn't verbalising.

'The food's good,' he said.

She washed down a slice of pizza with her beer.

'I think you're being a bit of a fucking riddler, Lahr – be straight with me, at least show me that much respect.'

'Fine, Emer. Those men are dangerous in Israel, in Lebanon, in Poland, in Ireland. If you mess with them, there will be consequences. I'm part of a civilian police force and so they'll think twice about coming after me, but if I get in their way, they'll...'

He paused.

'You, you're a soldier, a police soldier, what power do you have? What support? What have you got that would make them think twice about ending your life? Tell me.'

'So what do I do?'

'Write up the report when it's time.'

84

'You mean find no one amenable for the crimes and such nonsense; as in, if further information becomes available, a report will be submitted – lies?'

He eyed her steadily as though weighing his thoughts.

He said, 'The food is good.'

Lies. Casually uttered. She'd known a neighbour who'd lied about her son at her husband's grave, at a cemetery Mass, and a woman like that would lie about anyone anywhere, about anything.

'Lying can become an addiction, Lahr. You can develop a tongue that has many flyovers.'

'Pass the vinegar, would you?'

CHAPTER 15

She passed Caesarea, the location of the lost port of Herod, having crossed the border minutes before its electrified gates were swung closed and powered up. She'd gotten away later than planned. Lahr wanted to review statements, talk about case notes, and the likely trajectory of the investigation. He was piqued at Emer's stinging criticism of his light-touch leadership and she wondered if his concerns for her personal safety were genuine – good advice, for sure, but she couldn't prevent herself from wondering if it were flavoured with the tiniest undercurrent of threat.

She liked him. She admitted – yes – she found him encroaching on her thoughts more and more, wondering about him.

Her phone rang.

'Hi, Hannah, how are you?'

'You were absolutely brilliant on the telly last night – you looked really marvellous. The sun, and the sea behind you. Oh, it looked so divine. I pictured myself lying on the beach, going swimming. You lucky thing, you.'

'Hannah, the water is full of jellyfish and the beach is stony.'

'All the same, I would *adore* it.'

'Hannah... look, I...'

'What's up? Go on.'

'Nothing, nothing.'

I can't tell her, I can't worry her, I can't do that. She'd freak out and besides, they wouldn't, would they, go after her? They bloody well would...'

Hannah said, 'Are you okay?'

'Fine, really, I'm fine.'

'Where are you now, exactly? Tell me?'

'Just passing Akko.'

'Are you alone?'

'Yeah. Why?'

'Oh, so you can tell me all about the case?'

'No, I can't do that, sis, not over the phone.'

'Do you want to know what I think?'

'I'm not psychic, Hannah.'

Whenever her sister started this malarkey, Emer's natural tendency was to zone out.

'You are a little, Emer – Mam said you were born with the caul and people who do, have ESP, you know, extrasensory perception.'

'You're getting mixed up. It was her sister, *Aunt Emer*, who was born with the caul.'

'Oh.'

'And besides, everyone is a little psychic. It's called intuition.'

'Well anyway, Emer, that girl who's missing – do you think she might have run away?'

'We're keeping our minds open.'

While others like Sexton are keeping their lips sealed.

'I think she must have done,' Hannah said.

'I'll keep it in mind.'

'You know I'm good at this sort of thing, don't you?'

I do?

'She was being bullied, Emer. Mark my words.'

'Hmm.'

She got off the phone about five minutes later, after a prolonged series of goodbyes and at the last second... 'Oh, I forgot to tell you that Mandy Waters died.' And, 'Did I mention I was going for an interview?'

Hannah was scattered sometimes and quickly exhausted Emer's patience. Her sister was affable, quick to make friends, while Emer was more reserved in the company of strangers, and struggled to keep friendships, primarily because she wasn't good at maintaining contact and working at them. She was good with her own company, which seemed to annoy some people, who felt she should be more engaging. Coffee mornings with the girls and drinks out; such girly stuff she considered septic tank content: it wasn't in her nature. Her maternal instincts, too, according to her ex-rat of a husband, lay buried in the Sahara Desert. He was wrong. She'd love to have a child – she just wasn't sure if she wanted to rear one with a man. 'You've got huge trust issues,' Hannah had once told her.

True enough. She'd wrongly accused John of cheating on her, and he'd stared into her eyes and said there was no way he would cheat on her. 'No fucking way, Emer. I swear to God, I would never...' She kept her doubts lukewarm. No one could lie that convincingly, surely.

She came off the roundabout and eased her way into the heart of Netanya, parked in an underground car park. Going over in her mind was the suspicion that Nora Sexton and Jenny Casey were implicated in smuggling. It made sense and perhaps the beating Sexton sustained was because her comrades in crime believed that she had squared off on the figurine for herself. But one demon artefact or two or more? Is this why Casey was either dead or on the run? Was the relic deliberately hidden in the bus's luggage compartment? Or genuinely mislaid? Had the girls decided just to take one, for whatever reason?

Rumours. The TV interviewer had been in the country less than a few hours and heard the whisperings. The traders on the long street outside the UN Headquarters were good at sending out solid information but mixing it with lies and imaginings. Smuggling happened, a routine crime, but this was different. The traders, a few of these had obviously made a connection. How? They had ears on the ground – for God's sake, this was their turf. Why wouldn't some of them be in the know?

Morris had chewed the TV news anchor out for straying off script, but she wouldn't yield the name of her contact on the street. Emer had asked Pablo what he knew of the smuggling rumours and he shrugged, asked if she were happy with her pizza, if she and Lahr wanted more beer.

You hear all sorts of misinformation on the street, Lahr had said.

'Yeah,' she agreed, but thought, *Along with smidgens of truth*.

Lahr told her he was planning to interview Sexton today – in spite of the doctor's recommendation – then tomorrow to follow her into Israel, where he'd bunk in Jerusalem. This evening, he intended carrying out searches in the accommodation blocks where Quartermaster Hughie 'Smug' Boland and the Dabrowski brothers were quartered. Fredericksen's orders, he said.

Not your own decision, Lahr? Of course not.

'Do the Israelis know about the find?' she asked herself, alighting from the car.

Is Avi Cohen aware? Hardly.

Did Fredericksen brief him?

They'd driven from Israel into Lebanon with the figurine as bagged evidence. They were always searched crossing from Lebanon into Israel; the UN was never subjected to searches while going in the opposite direction. She supposed it made sense – things were dearer in Israel than they were in Lebanon. There was no economic sense in reverse smuggling.

It might be no harm for her to put Avi Cohen in the picture.

CHAPTER 16

otel Samuel's exterior gave her the feel of a place long surrendered to its ancient past; not seedy, simply neglected. Double doors, with red and blue stained-glass panels, opened up to a small rotunda. To her left was a marble-floor lounge with a corner bar and poorly arranged tan-coloured leather couches and walnut coffee tables.

At check-in, she was handed an old, heavy key to her room on the second floor.

Her mother's training was not lost on her; she'd brought along bed sheets, pillowcases, having got the notion Morris wouldn't have picked her a good hotel, not after reminding her to maintain a frugal grip on her expenses.

She opened the window and looked down at the narrow streetscape, Rue… something or other, she couldn't distinguish, as the street name was obscured by a tree's leafy branches. Emer turned, sighed. She always found a pervading sense of loneliness in hotels. Caused perhaps by the residual energy left behind by previous guests.

She cleared the dresser of its drinking glasses, maps, and brochures, and set her laptop to charge. Next to it she put the case file. Typing up statements and reports was tedious work she hated doing. Collating the material could be tricky, especially if she came across something needing clarification or handwriting almost impossible to decipher.

Grinding work, clocking three hours until she'd completed what she'd wanted to catch up on. Her mind was tired; she was hungry and thirsty for a beer. Wearily, massaging her neck, she got up from the chair, powered down her laptop, and slipped on a light blue jacket over her black T-shirt.

She paused, her fingers gripping the door handle, and looked at the spread of the work she was leaving behind. Felt a degree of satisfaction, and yet...

'I'm not seeing something,' she whispered. 'What is it?'

It won't come to me. Nuisance, she thought.

Emer asked for a recommendation from the receptionist. He suggested she turn right outside the hotel and after passing the nightclub she would come to a Chinese. Perfect food, if you liked Asian.

It was busy, but she found a seat at the bar and ordered. Then it hit her.

Should have checked for photos... got on Facebook... And then she remembered Lahr saying he was having that side of things looked into. But...

Had he actually attended to the matter?

She herself had forgotten.

What sort of a good cop has a bad memory?

Go sleep with the cockroaches.

She felt so tired. Drained.

Eat, sleep.

CHAPTER 17

The next morning, in bed drinking coffee, watching the news on TV, her phone sounded its bugle call.

It was Lahr. She silenced the TV.

'Hello,' he said, obviously on the move.

She said, 'How are things?'

'I interviewed Sexton yesterday and she wasn't very helpful. I think you might have a better chance of getting information from her. You should try once more.'

'Hmm. I don't think so. She doesn't like me. And you know that.'

So why suggest it?

She said, 'Did you check on the Facebook pages belonging to the touring party? You said you would.'

'Yes.'

'And?'

'If something had shown up, I would have told you.'

Really?

He went on, 'I have news for you about Casey's family. Her parents are coming out.'

Why wouldn't they? she thought.

'And also two detectives from the Irish civilian police.'

Well, we need all the help we can get, she supposed, in silence.

'They'll be here in a couple of days – Fredericksen would like us to have something positive by then.'

'Miracles do happen. I've been told this is the land for them.'

'I spoke with Morris and he said to tell you that he will ring you later.'

Probably about cutting short her stay in Israel, she speculated to herself, as there was no longer a need for her to push the case; the cavalry had arrived.

'Are you coming south anytime then?' she asked, thinking there wasn't a need for him here either.

'No, I'm collecting the detectives and Casey's family at Beirut Airport.'

'Perhaps the civil police should interview Sexton?'

'Maybe we should keep the case ours until we can't do that anymore.'

'Do you think?'

'What are you doing today?' he asked.

'I'm going to see Cohen; I'll call to the MP detachment afterwards and then sit down to sift through some more paperwork this evening.'

'Why not take a break? The heat is off you, yes, with the Irish coming out?'

Is the heat off me?

Shouldn't he have said 'us'?

CHAPTER 18

Avi Cohen was sitting behind his desk, waiting for her. His face so hard it could be abseiled. He wore a blue sleeveless shirt and scratched at a thin forest of dark hair along his forearm, on both of which were faded tattoos of Hebrew writing. He was slight and wirily built. Emer sensed he was not someone to underestimate – he was as menacing as the Dabrowskis, just in a different way that she had yet to experience.

He gestured for her to sit.

She averted her gaze to his freshly watered cacti and a grey vase of fresh sunflowers. She loved sunflowers, the image of their golden heads turning to worship the sun.

She took a breath and asked if the UN had informed him about the idol.

He hadn't heard.

'Which is not to say I didn't learn of it from another source.'

He joined his fingertips in a steeple.

The reason behind the hard face.

'Why did you not tell me this sooner?' he said.

'We thought it was merely an ornament, a piece of lost property – it might not have been lost by anyone on that particular group, but by someone else on another.'

'And now you know more, much more.'

'Yes, we had it examined.'

Cohen smoothed his hennaed hair, joined his hands, wrung them, cracked his knuckles.

Emer hated that particular habit; it played on her nerves.

'But,' he said, 'you or Timo Lahr, yes, did not think to tell me about this development.'

'I'm here to brief you on that today, Avi,' she said, 'and I had thought one of my superiors would have already notified you.'

'Hmm,' he uttered, not totally convinced.

He was edgier than a cat unable to claw open a can of tuna.

She handed him the glossy photograph of the figurine. He studied it and said, 'This puts a whole new perspective on the investigation – this piece was smuggled into Israel and then back out of it.'

'What are you saying?' Emer said.

'That we have a major problem at the border crossing – we and you, with people who are mine and yours.'

Apparently, Emer thought.

Cohen said, 'And six of these monstrosities make for the full set.'

'You know of them?'

'Of course. I have also been informed that they are hugely expensive items and have another value that is less intrinsic – they were used for ritualistic purposes, including human sacrifice. Probably used for that purpose alone.'

He sniffled, brought a mini fan to his face for a moment.

'In addition, I know of their origins – 3,000 years BCE. At least. They have been all around the Middle East – people have fought wars over them. The Iraqis kept imitations of them on display in their Baghdad museum, but looters with certain knowledge broke these into pieces and stole the authentic ones from the security basement. Along with a myriad of other ancient artefacts.'

'I have photos on my phone,' she said. 'There's a sort of writing on its back.'

'My son is a professor seconded to the Israel Museum. He briefed me – he said the script was one verse of a long chant, a call on the demon – it's why every figurine is needed for the ritual to be fulfilled. The six combine to allow the officiator to chant the entire thing.'

'The professor who read it, couldn't translate the piece – has your son managed to do that?'

'Show me,' he said.

She brought up the photos on her mobile phone and handed it over.

He nodded as he scanned and said, 'We will print a copy of them before you leave. I would like my son to see these. We have archival photographs but he believes those might be imitations.'

Silence.

'Is there anything else I should know?'

Emer appraised him of the pending arrival of Jenny Casey's parents, and members of the Irish civil police, the guards.

'What are your thoughts on the case?' he said, pointing at her with a blue Cross-brand pen – she used to have one like it.

She resented him for doing that and he knew, but nevertheless held his aim.

'It's obvious we have a smuggling problem. I think our soldiers have been involved in smuggling for some months, that the missing piece had probably been genuinely lost in the bus's luggage compartment. Either this possibility was overlooked or neglected in a search, or a presumption was made that it was stolen. This has something to do with Casey going missing. Abduction, most likely, or a forced flight. And as for Sexton's beating – I think the girls were suspected of stealing it. Whoever these pieces were destined for, well, it's fair to say he isn't someone to take lightly.'

'That's where you are at?' he said.

'So far. But I do have other thoughts that are not yet fully developed.'

'Very good,' he said, and paused. 'Very good.'

He sighed and then said, 'We have every sort of mad creature coming to our city – some perfectly sane people arrive here and,' clicked his fingers, 'turn into Christ – others search for the bones of Christ. We see all sorts. There are dangerous religious sects here, not just the ones that are constantly in your face.'

Emer smiled because she saw what he was driving at: the popular organised religions.

'There are underground sects, some we know of by word of mouth only. Whispers on the wind. So I'm focused on why someone would want to have these ugly relics in their possession, and I suspect they are not just for display in a glass cabinet.'

'They shield,' Emer said, 'against good angels trying to prevent souls being seized by Ba'al, I think. Evil feeds on the innocent, steals... energy... I read somewhere.'

'Specifically about these?'

'Not specifically those, no. It was a magazine article, a glossy. Gory reading for the most part.'

She'd confiscated the magazine during the hotel search.

'And that's what I'm afraid of,' Cohen said. 'Dead bodies turning up all over the city. My city. Unnecessary deaths due to some nonsense type of hocus-pocus. Pieces such as those need to be kept in a controlled and secure environment.'

'Those sorts of killings; have they happened already?'

'Not that I'm aware of. By the way, Ba'al is the Hebrew word for Lord – Christians call their Lord, Ba'al... A titbit of knowledge for you. Might as well call Christ, Satan.'

'Suit yourself.'

'Ah, a non-believer.'

*

'I believe money drove the apostles – want to run a successful

97

business? A good start would be to form a cult or spread word of an apparition, forge a miracle...'

'We shouldn't talk religion, eh? I can see that something has gravely embittered you.'

'I had a friend who prayed a lot for his mother to come home. She did, but not in the manner he'd prayed for.'

'Faith is tested by trials.'

'Hmm... Why was Roshaniqra chosen as a smuggling route?'

Avi shrugged. 'The sea is too well patrolled by the navy and airport security is extremely tight. So, a few corrupt UN soldiers, a few corrupt Israeli soldiers, someone who has connections with smugglers, someone, or some organisation with plenty of collateral and a belief in the occult found this route. It is almost like burying a body in a cemetery – the most obvious is sometimes the least obvious, is it not?'

'It's both brazen and daring, for sure,' she said.

'Have you factored in our only other border crossing with Lebanon, in Metula? You have MPs stationed there.'

'Are you telling me something?' she said.

'Only that it might be a sound consideration for you.'

Emer made a mental note to ring Lahr and advise him to ensure the demon figurine was in a lock-tight, secure location. Cohen's evaluation both disturbed and heightened her awareness – military police carried out searches of UN military and civilian staff at both crossings.

Emer watched Cohen get to his feet and walk to the window. Squinting between the slatted blinds at the blue skies of Jerusalem, he said, 'This worries me very much.'

CHAPTER 19

Emer delayed outside the MP detachment in Jerusalem to smoke and to mull over Avi Cohen's revelations, particularly about Metula. She hadn't considered that approach route. Had Lahr? He knew the area better; that was the Finnish battalion's sector. Rugged terrain, deep wadis, winding mountain roads. Neither the Finnish nor Norwegian battalions used the Roshaniqra border crossing to the south-east. Why would they, when Metula was much closer?

She was distracted by a raised voice and looked toward the green-netted window. Went close to it and saw Chief Joseph leaning over the seated Pedney, berating him, his features distorted. This was a side to the amiable Fijian chieftain she had not previously observed. Pedney appeared worried and harried; confused, too. She stubbed her cigar with her heel and went inside.

The chief's face slipped into a smile when he saw her, a different person to moments ago. Right now he was winging it with good humour he did not feel. He asked her how was the life, if she had enjoyed sleeping in his room; did she like the photographs of his family?

Emer sat on the sofa, crossed her legs. She wondered if Pedney had been caught in some sleazy behaviour again. She watched him as he filled the kettle at the sink, his back to them. A short man, skinny – in comparison Chief Joseph was a grizzly bear.

The chief flounced into the armchair opposite her. He smelled of coconut oil. Silver and gold rings adorned his thick fingers.

What is it with the men here? They all wear rings with stones.

He buttoned his shirt pocket as he said, 'Benny told me about the

99

case – it is very sad that the girl is still missing and the other girl has suffered very badly.'

'It is, yes. The trouble people make for themselves is sometimes astounding. Unfortunately, but...'

Silence.

'Speaking of Benny. Where is the staff sergeant?' Emer asked quietly.

'He has gone into town. Our other car is in Naqoura for service.'

Emer thought of irregularities with some of the logbooks. Mileage distances were not filled in correctly, if at all. Garage fills were recorded in a Paz book of duplicate slips; one given to the garage and the other left in the book. It was a nightmarish administration problem for the MP Company's transport sergeant.

I must give her a call, to query how this MP detachment is doing in that regard.

'How was your leave?' she asked.

'Okay, I worked in a kibbutz for the two weeks,' Chief Joseph said, 'picking oranges.'

'That's interesting, which kibbutz?'

'Outside Netanya, on the road to Akko.'

Hasn't it got a name? she thought.

Pedney brought the teapot and mugs, went to get the milk from the fridge. She gave a muted thanks, unable to bring herself to be too friendly. He was trouble heading for more. Fredericksen wanted him charged for lewd and indecent behaviour; Pedney had cupped a French soldier's breast as she'd slept, three months ago, and he was bound for Nepbatt, demoted. Justice is the slowest of slow runners.

She caught Chief Joseph's eye as he spooned sugar into his mug and asked, 'Have you been fully briefed on events?'

'Yes.' He nodded.

He stirred his coffee as though he were mixing heavy cement, laboriously.

'And you know what Pedney found in the luggage compartment?'

'The statue, yes.'

'Pedney,' she called, 'have you told anyone else about the discovery?'

She had to repeat herself for him to understand.

'Only you, ma'am, Lieutenant Lahr, Benny and...' He looked at Chief Joseph.

'We want to keep the news of the find as secret as possible,' Emer said. But she had the feeling the circle already had more perforations than a cheese grater.

A foreboding came to her, fuelled by an overwhelming sense that she had so much work to do, and had achieved so little.

She glanced at her watch, knocked back her tea and said, 'I didn't think it was this late. I have to be elsewhere.'

Pedney's look of concern at her announcement almost persuaded her to stay for a while longer. Whatever music Chief Joseph had sung into his ears, it had left him deeply disturbed.

CHAPTER 20

Morris called her at the hotel. She'd guessed right; he saw no sense keeping her in Israel now that the hotshot Irish police had arrived. Still, he'd paid for the hotel room in advance for five nights, so she may as well avail of the offer if she wanted, after which she could return to base. Bit her tongue against saying, 'Thanks but no thanks – it's far from the fecking Sherman.'

Emer felt restless. She needed to do something, force a break in the wall of silence and indifference. It was a spur-of-the-moment decision for her to cross the border into Lebanon. A gut instinct that a second thought couldn't dispel.

On the trip north to Roshaniqra Border, she turned up the air conditioning and enjoyed the view of the sandy beaches – of palm trees dancing with a southerly breeze. Her mind turned over the scene she'd witnessed through the window in Jerusalem.

Emer wasn't sure if Pedney's nature was an issue with Chief Joseph.

Something else about Pedney's confused and fearful expression scratched at her bones. Yes, his eyes were as his roaming hands; his English poor, his cooking skills zero – yet she felt a little sorry for him. His fellow military police kept him confined to the detachment – perhaps rightly so, giving his predilection. When he was brought along to assist with the searches at the hotel, he'd been amazed. Thrilled to be let out – like a puppy seeing his master producing a lead, he was beside himself.

She wondered when he was due back in Headquarters. Perhaps it would be no harm to have someone speak with him on the quiet, in his own language. The predecessors of that particular detachment had all been recalled early, for partying instead of performing their duties... Maybe there was a lingering, more deep-rooted problem there?

Or was she just scrutinising everything to distract her from brooding on the feelings she had concerning the investigation? Where was the sense of urgency? At least the Israelis were keeping their word, with TV and radio announcements about the missing soldier. In reality, what did the lack of UN urgency mean in this instance? Ineptitude, probably. Bureaucracy – the system is ponderous and moves like a blindfolded sheep oblivious to stepping on its own dirt.

Did Lahr suss it correctly? She was inexperienced. Doing well, in spite of that fact.

Jenny Casey was gone. Rushing around wasn't going to find her any quicker. The cold light of the truth is that she was most likely dead.

And perhaps what I'm really feeling, she thought, *is a seam of anger at the notion that Casey's UN comrades – and mine, too – hold the four aces in the deck.*

Feck this. I'm going to give Corporal Sexton a shake; the medical people can whine.

CHAPTER 21

UNIFIL Hospital was a large complex of interconnecting prefabs near to the harbour just outside the UN camp. Sad-looking palm trees, leaves dust drenched, flanked her as she headed to the car park. She passed the helipad, the letter 'H' on the landing zone read as a lower-case 'h', the capital letter time-eroded. Before she could enter Sexton's private room, she introduced herself to the doctor who reluctantly gave his consent, told her ten minutes max, and no upsetting of the patient. She was vulnerable and her bloods were not quite right.

Yeah, yeah, she thought. *I'm not going to pull her teeth; she shouldn't need an anaesthetic to be truthful.*

Sexton eyed her cautiously.

Emer half-smiled as she brought a chair close to the bed.

Her eye had caught the windowsill and a vase of yellow flowers in a beige vase, off which paraded a line of get-well cards.

'Do you mind?' she said, already reading the names on the cards, some of which held many names and loads of 'x's, 'miss you' and so on.

No get-well wishes from the Poles. From Boland, yes. No 'x', though.

'They're lovely,' she said, smelling the flowers. 'What are they called?'

No answer.

'I'm not a flower name person either, apart from the easy-to-remember types, roses and that,' Emer said, as she sat down.

'Can I get you some water, a Pepsi, something?' she said.

Sexton looked away.

'Nora, you know, we do need to have a serious talk.'

The corporal turned her head. Emer saw a slight improvement in her condition; her face was still bruised, her hair – a bald patch she hadn't noticed before, above her temple.

'How are you feeling?' Emer queried. 'You are looking a little better than when I last saw you in Jerusalem.'

No answer.

'Nora?'

The patient's eyes were on the opposite light blue wall, as though she was fixing her gaze on a spot there. Emer recognised the blocking-out tactic.

'I have nothing to say. I can't remember anything,' Corporal Nora Sexton said, faintly.

There was the abrupt firing of a shotgun from outside, startling both. MP feline killers on the prowl, culling wild cats in response to a request by the Medical Commanding Officer, Emer explained.

Sexton's bruises were on the cusp of changing colour, and the swelling of her jaw and lip would soon begin to diminish. She told Sexton this in an attempt to find a way into the questioning process, to avoid the dogged route. Time was a factor, though.

Emer had expected to see more of an improvement but reminded herself that the beating was merely days old.

'I see that your husband is due to arrive tomorrow, along with Jenny's parents,' Emer said.

Sexton did not respond.

'And the Garda detectives,' Emer said.

A light creasing at the corners of her eyes, Emer observed.

'You might want to discuss the happenings with Jenny's parents and the guards. They'll be anxious to hear what it is that you have to say.'

'I can't remember. I've told you.'

'You can remember to tell me that you can't remember – I'm sure the guards will try to jog your memory,' Emer said, continuing in a gentle tone. 'Everything will come out in the wash, Nora.'

No response.

Emer said, 'Okay... I'm happy that I've tried my best with you. I need to pee and you need to think about how you're going to explain to the military bosses how an illegal substance got into your blood. And I'm sure that your husband will want to know how you lost your baby. Not his, but yours and whoever else's it was.'

Emer rose a little from the chair.

Do you know what? she thought. *Her silence makes it easier. I can simply write 'non-cooperation' in my report. Step back a little, Lahr's advice.*

'I have a kid at home,' Sexton said in a low tone. 'He's only three.'

Emer sat down, expecting to hear more. When she didn't, she said, 'Why are you telling me that? Do you think that's going to stop me from briefing – what's his name? – David, about your flings with Lukas and Hughie? And whoever else?'

Sexton closed her eyes.

Emer stood straight and said, 'I'm off to the loo. When I come back and you're still singing dumb, I'm off.'

As it turned out, Emer later reflected, she could have been peeing 24/7 and Sexton wouldn't have touted, for while Emer was away she had slit her wrist.

CHAPTER 22

About an hour after the attempted suicide, Emer was sitting with Lahr in Fredericksen's office. Morris was on his way. They drank from bottles of water and Lahr had looked at her several times, as though he'd something he wanted to get off his chest. His greeting to her had been cool, distant. She trawled through her memory banks to see if she had said something to alienate him. Nope. So he must be vexed with her for making a complete disaster of the Sexton interview. Which, she believed, was also the reason why Morris was breaking his neck to get back from Tyre: to chew on her ear. 'It's all happening,' she would later say to Hannah.

Yet, she hadn't leaned so hard on Sexton, had she? She didn't think so. But...

'Brief us as to what exactly happened, Captain Harte,' Fredericksen said, as a furious Morris entered. He leaned against the desk, keeping his eyes from engaging with Emer's. She spoke quietly, referring once to her notebook – to escape their attention, more so than to glean information – to say she had no idea that Sexton was suicidal.

'You were too bloody hard on her,' Colonel Gerry Morris uttered.

'I asked her the questions that others intend to ask and most certainly will.'

'Would have done,' Morris corrected. 'Hardly now, at least not for some time.'

'I did suggest we leave it to the Irish detectives,' she said, looking toward Lahr for support.

'You induced her with a threat,' Morris said, his cheeks plum coloured with anger.

'Who told you that?'

'Does it matter?'

'Of course, the source of your information is important.'

Fredericksen motioned with his hands. 'Enough.'

'I didn't get a chance to make an inducement,' Emer said.

'Oh, so you admit you were going to make one?' Morris said, almost sneeringly.

'I'd have said anything, promised her anything if I thought it would give me even a half an idea as to Casey's whereabouts. We need to find her fast. Every hour that passes decreases our chances of finding her, dead or alive.'

'I love the drama,' Morris said.

'With all due respect, sir – this is no drama at play, just a life-and-death situation.'

Fredericksen signalled to smother Morris's response. Morris's lips clammed so tightly that Emer saw the lines about them sink deeply, sinkholes of the flesh.

'Yes, you are correct,' Fredericksen said. 'That is our priority – to locate this missing soldier. Occasionally, Colonel Morris, we police officers have to stray into the dark for reasons of greater good and purpose. The issue of legality can be argued over at a later date.'

Lahr said, 'We now know one thing for certain: she's absolutely in fear for her life and the lives of her family.'

Emer felt the shadow of her own fear graze her neck. In Lahr, she saw some apprehension – for her? Himself? Both?

Morris spoke, exhaustion showing in the arcs under his eyes. 'How do I explain this situation to her husband? Her cutting her wrist after being visited by an officer investigating the case?'

Clearly and succinctly, colder than she intended, Emer said, 'She's still alive. She didn't cut out her tongue. She can explain everything to him. In fact, we should consider interviewing him to determine if she revealed what she knows of the incident...'

Morris nodded slowly, surprised somewhat at the steel in Emer's tone.

'After all,' she went on, 'he is military too – a comrade soldier of his is missing. In the event that she does reveal anything, he needs to be reminded that he is duty bound to pass it on to us.'

'Will you inform him about the miscarriage, her affairs?' Lahr said, eyes on the biro he held.

'I don't think it a good idea – we now know her mental and emotional state, how traumatised she is. As you put it – scared out of her skin.'

'Should we also be concerned for ourselves and our personnel?' Fredericksen asked.

'We're digging for truths,' Emer said, 'and yes – regarding the smuggling aspect, the discovery of that figurine, we have no idea what else we'll uproot. The Israelis are upping their interest. We have military police who are smuggling into Israel or at the very least turning a blind eye to it.'

'Hmm,' Lahr mulled.

'For Avi Cohen,' she went on, 'it's no longer a missing person case. He sees far more reaching consequences.'

'Such as?' Morris queried.

'That someone is planning to bring the six figurines together. These relics have a religious significance – occult and ritualistic. According to Cohen, that is. He says they're dealing with a wealthy individual or a group most likely that has wealth and a cause.'

'The occult,' Fredericksen said, the latter word playing on his lips as though it were a joke, one that for the life of him he could not seriously entertain.

Emer explained, 'These are figurines that Cohen calls devices. They are used in a death ritual to ensnare and enslave the soul of an innocent – a lunatic fringe, for sure, sir. The Israelis don't want this happening in their backyard – they've already got enough problems to contend with.'

Morris snapped, 'Daft nonsense.'

'Daft, yes – but we're in its world now,' Emer said, 'with an idol in our possession.'

Fredericksen said, 'Who else knows of its location?'

'Emer. And you, sir,' said Lahr, addressing his superior.

Fredericksen studied Morris for seconds until his look became crystal clear. Morris left the room. It was now solely a police briefing.

Fredericksen drummed his fingertips on the desk and then said, 'Okay, this is what is going to happen. You will bring the statue to Tyre this evening and hand it over to Iraqi personnel – there will be two of their officials from their National Museum in Baghdad: a curator and a professor of antiquities. A security team will accompany them. The Force Commander has decided this.' He handed Lahr a business card. 'This is your contact number if things go wrong and there's a delay. They'll be waiting for you at that restaurant in the city's Maronite sector.'

Cloak and dagger, Emer thought. *A good idea though, to have that creepy little blue demon far from the company lines.* She liked that about Fredericksen; the way he hadn't sat on this issue; that he could haul his ass when he wanted.

'You should leave within the next hour and wait for their arrival at the restaurant. I'll ring them to expect you.'

Lahr and Emer glanced at each other. They were in the worry woods, as G.I. used to call problems.

Emer said, 'Should we take an escort?'

'No,' Fredericksen said. 'This operation has to be watertight. Who else can we trust? We don't have the resources either. The SIS section is busy the next two days with searching and policing the Nepalese and Ghanaian homeward rotations. This way is better.'

After leaving the office, they went to the Duty Room to sign out their personal firearms. Lahr said with laboured casualness, 'I have other news for you.'

'What?'

'I'm leaving for Finland tomorrow evening.'

She drew up short. He half-turned to her.

'Leaving? Is everything okay at home?'

He coughed, averted his eyes. 'I think so... I am going on leave to find out.'

In her, a rage flared like a forest fire.

'Our colonel cleared it – because the Irish police are here – and we're getting rid of the relic this evening.'

'Relic? You're the blooming relic, you tool. You knew about this meet-up in Tyre before I did...'

He smiled, lost it under her glare.

'What?' he said.

'I had my leave cancelled, remember?'

'It's still an Irish case. And my leave is compassionate.'

The reason didn't impact with her, still angry.

'Bull. You're the officer in charge of the investigation. You shouldn't just get to walk away.'

'My daughter has been crying on the phone for me to come home,' he said, his voice cracking. 'My mother is extremely worried about her.'

There was nothing left for her to say. Her anger was snuffed out like a birthday candle.

CHAPTER 23

Emer left Lahr to sign out his weapon and went to see the Transport NCO in her office. The young sergeant's monthly transport returns were due to be sent to HQ and they were in a mess.

She gestured to the pile of documents on her desk, pointed to the spreadsheet on her computer and muttered aloud a familiar argument to Emer.

'Are they so stupid that they cannot do simple math, or do they do it deliberately to mess with my head?'

'Both,' Emer said.

'I mean, you write the mileage on the clock before you start, and when your journey is finished, then you subtract and get your mileage. They don't do this for a few days and everything is guesswork then – different drivers...' she said, sighing with frustration.

Silence.

'Frances. I have a big ask of you.'

'Oh. Okay.'

She asked if she would check the records of Polish Logistics, in relation to the touring party's driver. Lukas Dabrowski? Find the locations of his gas fills in the Leb and in Israel, destinations and so on; say, for the previous month? Do it without Pollog getting wind of it. Also, any Jerusalem MPs, try to figure out as much from the mess of their log reports as possible. Perhaps they tripped over their stupidity by trying to box too clever.

Frances stared at the pile of paperwork with a hunted look and gave a slight nod.

CHAPTER 24

While she gave a quick cleaning to her Browning pistol in the armoury, Lahr went to the investigation office and fetched the idol from the evidence safe.

'You have the little creep?' she said, her eyes on his green travel bag as he edged past her in the narrow armoury, to his locker. She caught the faint scent of his aftershave as he squeezed past, his hand lightly on her shoulder. His touch aroused her a little; it had taken her by surprise. A light touch.

'Yes,' he replied.

He watched her run an oil rag over the pistol, drying it well, so dust wouldn't interfere with its mechanism. She poured her angst into cleaning the pistol, trying to shake her mood. She felt a little guilty over how she'd pushed Sexton into slitting her wrist. Fine, yeah, to tell herself it would have happened anyway, as someone else was going to drop the questions onto her head. But it'd happened on her watch. Nor had she stopped to think about what was going on in Lahr's life. His daughter was sick, he'd told her this before, and perhaps he was flying home to hear bad news, or deal with it? So much of it would explain his handling of the case thus far: he had far more pressing matters.

What sort of person am I?

Christ. I'm on Sexton's side. On Lahr's, too.

But they made her feel that she wasn't.

The nine bullets on her table during her pistol's cleaning process were not as ugly as the idol – yet these small brass pieces were designed to spin through flesh and break bone to smithereens. In turn, these spinning shards of bone would slice internal organs to ribbons. True evil would sit, in the next minute or so, in the box magazine housed in her pistol.

Armed in seconds: the slide drawn back, then freed, safety catch released, the squeeze of her finger pad on the trigger. A person's world can change in that slow inhalation, exhalation.

Am I trying to convince myself of something here?

The idol freaks me the hell out.

In comparison, the brass rounds, their capacity to create mayhem and destruction, held a small chill for her. A bullet once spent, is lost. This artefact, how many lives had it observed being taken during some deadly chant?

After inserting the magazine into the weapon's handle, she holstered the Browning and put on her web belt, then clipped the lanyard to the pistol's loop.

*

Outside the gates, they veered left to travel north along the coastal road. At about 3km, they passed a military police speed and documentation checkpoint, their patrol vehicle parked in the yard of a derelict house next to a rock face with a cave entrance.

She waved. The MPs waved. Lahr hadn't. His hands white-knuckled on the wheel.

'The road's quiet,' she remarked.

'It always is around this time,' he said.

'In fact, it's empty.'

'Yes, but I don't think it strange, not at this hour.'

'I've never seen this road without traffic.'

He said nothing.

The sun bounced off waters in bursts of silvery light and the white teeth cut hard against the rocky shoreline. Rounding the bend, they could see the isthmus of Tyre, originally created by Alexander the Great, the causeway helping his army to finally break the city's siege. He had crucified the inhabitants along the reach of the shore, punishment for holding out so long, delaying his military expedition to East Asia.

Lahr was silent, shades on, shoulders raised.

A burst of static erupted from the Cruiser's radio.

She wanted to say something but wasn't sure what. She wasn't good at small talk. He hadn't opened up to her and she didn't want him to think she was prying.

It doesn't help that every second sentence out of my mouth these days is a question.

She decided upon the most inoffensive of enquiries. 'Are you okay?'

Space enough if he wanted to push words through.

'I'm fine, thanks.'

Tersely said.

Oh, leave him the hell alone.

'I'm looking forward to eating in that restaurant in Tyre,' she said, trying once more. 'I'm famished. A tuna. I'll have tuna. You?'

Not a peep from him.

Ah, F him.

She saw a UN car ahead with its front wheel jacked up, a puncture.

Emer tensed.

'Where's the driver?' she asked, looking at Lahr. 'Drive on by,' Emer added, sensing it was the right course of action.

But Lahr, as she spoke, was already pulling over in front of the soft-skinned vehicle, keeping about three metres distance between bonnets. The sea breeze blew hard against its grimy white canopy and pulled at its ties. Emer tugged on her holster's buckle, eased her hand over the black handle, gripped tightly and drew out the pistol. Cocked it.

Lahr said with calmness fused with alarm, 'There is no need for that.' Reaching in the back for his travel bag, he said, 'This is what they want.'

'Lahr, the shit like. What the fucking hell do you think you're doing?'

'I'll explain later. You'll have to trust me on this. I want to keep us both alive. You've got a death threat hanging over your head – you know this. I so badly need the money for my little girl.'

He got out and began to approach the other vehicle, cradling his travel bag in the crook of his arm.

Her gut instinct had been in tune. She hadn't noticed a wheel brace – had thought she was being overly cautious. The driver needed to borrow a brace, that's all. She relaxed a little but felt as though she were conning herself into believing she'd been jumpy for no good reason.

She breathed in the salt air, let the breath go.

Lahr disappeared around the rear of the other car.

This is a total mess.

Moments later he showed, his hands raised above his head. The blood drained from his face. He half-stumbled toward her, pushed into a forward motion. She couldn't see who was behind him, a weapon being used to herd him.

A metre from the windscreen, he stopped and said loudly, 'They're not wearing masks. They were supposed...'

A bang, the bullet report sharp and resounding. She saw him fall in a heap. And Dabrowski, now in full view, took aim at her with an assault rifle. She lowered her head just as the windscreen shattered on top of her. Four, five rounds zipped above her, ripping through the upholstery, slamming into metal, piercing the rear-end passenger windows.

Silence.

Is this it? Am I finished?

There was a wheezing in her harsh breathing, the suspirations of a valve leaking air. Her ears rang. She slipped head-first from her seat onto the dirt, her palm and the side of her gun hand resting on pieces of sharp window glass. Gritted her teeth against the pain.

Why has he stopped shooting?

Is Lahr dead?

She heard the shooter changing magazines or clearing a jam, in no hurry, the mechanical movements lazily done.

'Are you sure you hit her?'

She recognised the voice. Boland.

'You look. Go on, Irish.'

Emer thumbed the safety down, fired two rounds under the Cruiser's chassis, catching Lahr's shooter in the shins. He roared. She released two more, in anger, in terror, as he lay writhing on the ground. Emer crawled to the back of the Cruiser, her training kicking in; crawl, cover, observe. Fire?

She got to her hunkers, peered from behind the brake lights at Boland staring in disbelief at the man she'd just shot.

He said, 'Jesus. Sweet Jesus.'

He was armed with a pistol.

Nervously, he kept glancing behind and ahead for approaching traffic. None was coming from either direction. She thought of the MP checkpoint... delaying traffic, holding it up... and maybe similar was happening to the north.

'Put the pistol down,' Emer shouted, from cover.

Blood trickled from her forehead, oozed into her right eye and stung. She closed it tightly. He made a move. Emer fired a warning shot above his head. She could taste her own blood and spat out a nugget of sharp windscreen glass.

Boland fired. The round tore through a side mirror and sparked against the wheel nearest her head, centimetres away. Flying metal, a screeching banshee wail. Emer crab-walked to the passenger side of her vehicle and surprised him. As he turned she discharged two rounds, instantly dropping Boland to his knees. He was clutching his upper arm, trying to stem the geyser of blood. He groaned, danced a jig on his knees, bit at his lower lip.

She lowered her pistol, let it drop from her hand. It fell to close her ankle, held by the lanyard. Boland tried to stand but couldn't. Comical to look at, almost, she thought.

Lahr's eyes took in the living skies, his hands extended as though he were about to embrace a loved one. Dabrowski lay close to him, his chest heaving up and down, bleeding profusely. He whispered for help.

She turned from the scene, went to the side of the road, and threw up over the guardrail, squatted for a few moments and then sat down on the red earth. Shock surged like nausea through her. Her eyes far-off, watching the horizon through bloodied eyes.

CHAPTER 25

Emer's eyes followed the second hand on the wall clock. She was seated on a gurney at UNIFIL Hospital. Alone. Minutes earlier, a nurse had washed her cuts and grazes, bandaged her left hand.

A lucky woman. Lucky to be alive.

Tick-tock.

Tick-tock.

A loud burst of commotion emanated from outside. Polish voices, busy trying to save someone's life, telling each other the must-dos. Lahr's? She prayed – if 'Sweet Jesus' could be described as a prayer.

Tick-tock.

She wanted to look at herself in a mirror, to scrutinise her injuries. Nothing to worry about, the nurse said. But her eyes, she wanted to see their colour, that the whites held no flecks of blood. She wished she were able to soak her eyes in a basin of warm and salted water, so she would know for sure they were clean. She wished to erase a patch of memory. To reduce what had happened to nightmare status, a clutter of bad dreams in which no one really dies.

A tear fell.

She saw Lahr take the bullet. Saw his expression, saw him collapse...

Before that, she'd witnessed his coming toward her in a pallor of shock. In that moment, he had come to understand so much. The very instant he'd handed over the idol, when he saw Dabrowski and Boland wearing no masks, he'd learned. They'd reneged, had probably intended all along to kill any witnesses. This time. Jenny

Case was simply a worry they'd yet to extinguish.

Bastards.

Lahr, you… she thought. *What were you at? Saving me, saving your daughter? What else? You jennet.*

She shook her head and pinched her wrist to prevent herself from crying, using physical pain to stem the flow. She continued to sit there, though every part of her wanted to move. Just move. To walk away. A coldness surged through her veins as she tried to think about nothing.

Lucky woman?

CHAPTER 26

About an hour and a half after her discharge from hospital, Fredericksen handed her a large, hot whiskey in the MP mess. Not a word seemed alive on their tongues. She had just finished briefing them about the ambush. Fredericksen himself had led the investigation team. Photographed the scene and videoed the after-images of mayhem: the bullet-punctured vehicle, empty shell casings counted, vehicle position triangulated and sketched. Later, the evidence bagged and removed. Red rivulets and splotches of red – the detritus of conflict hosed by a clean-up crew; flushed under the guard rails, down the scrubby incline onto the rocky shore.

Colonel Gerry Morris entered the silent lounge and spoke gently to Emer. 'How are you?'

She nodded, issued an almost inaudible sob. Unable to verbalise a response, throat cords like vines choking each other.

Fredericksen said into the gloom. 'Boland?'

'He'll live,' Morris replied, and added, 'Dabrowski has a sixty per cent chance.'

'I've been in touch with Sadimaki and he's going to notify Lahr's family,' Fredericksen said, raising his whiskey glass.

After smacking his lips, he said, 'He might pull through, but they're far more hopeful than certain.'

Morris's sigh was loud and protracted.

'The press are starving wolves out for news,' Fredericksen said, running his hand over his cropped hair. 'I'm considering saying that there was a traffic accident on the coastal road between UNIFIL Headquarters and Tyre, which resulted in serious injuries.'

'A traffic accident,' Emer said, deeply puzzled.

'For now.' Fredericksen's expression made it clear the situation was fluid and everyone was struggling to come to terms with what had happened. 'Emer,' he continued, 'I know this is not a question you want to hear, not right now, but I must ask. The idol of Ur is missing.'

Emer, through bleary eyes. 'It was in Lahr's travel bag, in the Jeep; he gave it to the Pole.'

Silence.

She shook her head and said, 'So, where is it? Who...'

Fredericksen said, 'That's what we intend to find out.'

'Who reported the incident?' she asked, before taking to her whiskey.

Fredericksen replied, 'The firing was heard by our own road traffic MPs and Israeli soldiers from their clifftop base. Both rang our Operations office to see if we were aware of it. When we got there, we found a crowd of onlookers – by then you were in the back of the ambulance.'

Silence.

Morris said, 'Can you go over what happened once more, take us from the time you left here?'

She swallowed some more whiskey, not allowing time for its flavour to rest on her palate, and began.

Lahr. It had to be you who leaked where we were headed and why.

I'm not going to lie or cover up for you in any way.

CHAPTER 27

The evening ran into a long night and into the early morning hours. She went over the story again and then once more. Fredericksen and the investigation team wanted to pick up on any discrepancies in her retell, but they also knew her talking would help the psychological healing process.

The assailants' Jeep wasn't found at the scene. She could not recall its registration plate number, only the model type and its grimy canopy. An old vehicle. Could have been stolen years ago by one of the factions in Lebanon for use as a suicide bomb vehicle, to trick the Israelis into thinking it belonged to the UN; that was Fredericksen's theory.

Lahr's involvement in the proceedings hugely startled and disappointed Fredericksen. Morris's reaction was less revealing: he'd no business being involved in the investigation, and so she gathered his interest was solely towards her, because she was Irish, and because of Casey.

He hadn't much of an input but suggested Fredericksen reconsider his traffic accident press release. Bluntly added he couldn't understand where the hell he was going with that notion.

Fredericksen agreed with a long, solemn nod, decided against his earlier intention, and changed the wording of the press briefing to read of an ambush perpetrated against UN troops, leaving two soldiers fighting for their lives, and a third with serious life-changing injuries. Scant information but it pushed the posse in another direction; which terrorist organisation had ambushed the UN soldiers? An attack on peacekeepers – not peace enforcers – was generally viewed by the public as cowardly.

It dawned on her as to why her commanding officer was inclined to mislead others about the true circumstances. Was it ingrained in him to protect and preserve reputation – anything that would sully the name of UNIFIL or his own unit while on his watch? Police circled the wagons when they felt their good name was under threat. Something to note for future reference, she thought.

The press release furnished no names, no unit, merely enough bones to appease a media hungry for information, who themselves were already using other sources to dig for answers.

Morris advised her to slip across into Israel, to the hotel in Netanya; get away for a few days and try to rope her thoughts together. And if she needed anything, not to hesitate in giving him a call. If she wanted company, did she know of anyone?

'I'll be all right.'

She left directly from the club with Fredericksen's blessing and his warning for her to lie low.

CHAPTER 28

In her hotel room three nights later, she took a shot of whiskey to help slide the sleeping pill, then extracted the last pull of her cigar before snuffing it dead in a brass ashtray supported by brown plastic camels. She badly needed to get some sleep, to be in some sort of decent shape to deal with what was ahead of her. Wanted to sleep so she could forget, abandon the speeding carousel of her thoughts. Respite. Please.

When sleep eventually arrived she dreamt of Lahr's remains receiving a military send-off from Beirut Airport. It rained through the sunshine. Clouds were dark on the Chouf Mountains.

Her phone dragged her out from drowsiness, zombie on the rise and said, in spite of a voice in her skull saying for her not to, 'Hi.'

Hannah asked how she was.

'Not good... You?'

'What's the matter?'

'Belly, too much hummus. Any news?'

'I'm going with a friend to see someone we know perform in a play – she's playing a mute and we can't wait to see her go for an hour and whatever without speaking.'

'Sounds interesting.'

'God. You sound a bit down.'

'I've got a bug,' she lied. 'Believe me, Hannah, it would stop an elephant in its tracks.'

'What are you taking for it?'

'Everything bar the kitchen sink.'

'You poor thing.'

'I'll be grand in a day or so.'

Hannah asked about the missing Jenny Casey.

Emer did not prolong the conversation any more than necessary and said she'd call soon. Hannah was easily huffed because she could read between the lines, and resented the brush-off – after all, they were sisters. She would assume she had every right to know.

The latest press update would scarcely create a ripple in the media waters back home. When news of the shootout surfaced, they'd want to air it big-time. Make her out to be the Irish *Annie Oakley*, the American markswoman. If and when Lahr died – that's what it looked like, a matter of when and not if – it would come out... as she had said to Sexton... in the wash.

It was not only for Lahr that she sometimes cried. Emer shed them for his daughter, his mother, for anyone who had known and liked him, who would miss him.

Her tears were for herself, too. She'd come very close to being placed on a mortuary slab – people had tried to murder her. The memory made her stomach bunch into a tight knot.

A troubled version of came, with a dead man smiling, teasing her about her scar and its likeness to his pet dog.

And Dad and Mam were there, too. Horseracing, just home after backing a winner, smiling. Images she remembered when she woke up, in the moments before sliding back into sleep.

CHAPTER 29

Xanax pills held her together. She did not like popping them, even rarely, but they helped in a crisis situation, so her transport sergeant Frances asserted as she discreetly fed them onto her palm in the MP Club.

Days ago, the shooting, the theft of life and artefact. The images and smells of that day would haunt her for the rest of her life. Sages say that the past is dead time, to move on from it, and yet the past lived with her in the present and for the future too, for sure. Dead time it is not. She didn't think it possible to quickly move on from a crisis such as this – it would take more than a single leap. Stepping stones. But these were a luxury...

Distractions help.

She considered whether the Israelis were clued into what had happened. They had spies everywhere – human and advanced technology. Drones swept Lebanon for anything remotely resembling military activity.

Should she call Avi Cohen?

She kept her phone turned off, only giving it a window for an hour in the evening. She was drinking heavily, smoking cigars, and had even gone through a pack of Camel cigarettes in a day. She slept most of the morning, some days well into the afternoon. Ate little, sometimes in a Greek restaurant, served by the same waiter, who removed the opposite cutlery and crockery. His simple action only amplified her loneliness and sense of isolation.

Six days in exile, then they sent for her.

Morris asked to Skype but she looked a mess and her sober voice was a lie to the rest of her. She was all out of clean bras and knickers and her period had arrived early.

No, she wanted no one to see her, and she to see no one.

Career. Life. As far as she was concerned, it was dog devour bitch and bitch eat dog.

'I'll pay my way here for a few more days,' she said, thinking he'd called to remind her that it was time to return the key.

'Don't worry about that, Emer. I can't say too much over the phone. But there's been a huge breakthrough concerning Casey.'

It didn't break her inertia.

'Do you know what? I'm going home,' she said, as she put one leg into her denim cargos.

'Get up here as soon as possible, and we'll talk then.'

She muttered, 'Sir,' and hung up.

Emer dwelled for minutes with her thoughts and then made for the shop down the road from the hotel to buy herself some underwear, sanitary towels – she hated using inserts – and a vanilla ice cream with a chocolate Flake, maybe two.

Maybe even a haircut, a tidy-up; there wasn't much to trim. Still, it might give her a bit of a lift. Might distract her, might cloud over the images of the shootout. Sepia pictures of Wyatt Earp and the OK Corral flew into her mind. But only the bad guys had died in that one – if she remembered correctly. Then, in the heel of the hunt, Lahr was a bad guy.

The sun cut against her eyes as she walked, a dog cocked its leg against a sorry-looking palm tree, and a bus driver honked wildly at an errant cyclist. Should have brought the sunglasses. *Going home*, she thought. *Not a bloody bad idea at all.*

She was lying to herself, she knew.

She would only go home if sent.

Emer hoped she'd have no choice.

CHAPTER 30

After leaving the salon, she went to Hamzo's and ate a Caesar salad and a well-done minute steak with a side dish of skinny paprika-dressed fries, washed down by Maccabi lagers.

Disinclined to park herself in the hotel room for the remainder of the evening, she stayed under a café's blue awning, decided on another beer, a Budweiser this time, and lit up a cigarillo. Watched people and traffic pass by, with *The Jerusalem Post* folded at her elbow. In truth, she paid it scant attention, a mere sanctuary for her eyes when she tired of looking around.

Emer recalled the interview with Avi Cohen. He had asked her what the MPs intended to do about the Dabrowski brothers, Lukas and Janus – or the Fox, as Benny had called the latter. She had said nothing at the time because they were already mired in a serious investigation, and resources were stretched. It'd have to be passed up the line for her superiors to decide on a course of action.

If they had lifted the brothers, would Lahr be in a coma? Would an attack have occurred? How deep was Lahr's own involvement? She ran the ambush in her mind's eye, thinking of how the Jeep was no surprise to him, nor the empty road along the way. The only surprise he showed, was when he was being pushed toward her. His complexion grey, drawn, pained. No masks. No balaclavas. He had understood their meaning only too easily.

Home?

Will they repatriate me?

She asked herself this question, fanning smoke from her face. Who had taken the idol?

Were people hurt for my antagonising of the Poles?

Her phone beeped.

Text. Hannah.

'Can u ring, sis? If ur not bsy.'

Not busy. Of course, not. Just going mental, sis.

'Hi, Hannah.'

'I heard you were involved in a shootout. What the hell are you involved with?'

'How did you find out?'

'The papers. Your name isn't mentioned, Emer, but I know it's you... Are you okay? Why the fuck didn't you tell me?'

'I'm sworn to secrecy.'

Not to mention, she thought, *your life is under threat, too.*

Tell her?

No. Not until I'm absolutely certain it is.

But if it weren't before, it is now – because I shot a Dabrowski.

'Oh, well thank you, Emer, very much. I'm only your sister. Your only bloody sibling. I thought we told each other everything.'

'Hannah.'

'What?'

'I've got something to tell you... and I need you to listen very carefully.'

After Emer finished speaking, a silence took root.

'Oh my god, are you serious?' Hannah said. 'Me. Me! Me who never did any flipping thing to anyone.'

'Yes. So listen to the advice that I'm going to give you and follow it to the letter.'

'John was so right, you should have left the army. Look at the shit you've gotten us, me, into. And—'

She clicked Hannah off and picked up her glass.

Another beer.

Five, in all, and two shots of whiskey.

Hotel.

A little unsteadily on her feet, down the poorly lit alley, right at the top, a few strides more to the hotel entrance.

She sat in the lobby, trying to stop herself from excavating hurt, picking over things like a child nervously pulling at the corners of a Band Aid.

'Miss Harte?' a man's tinny voice said from behind a tiny reception desk, almost across from her.

She coughed and said, 'Yes, Charlo?'

'Something left, a parcel here for you.'

Something, she thought.

Wiping her lips with the back of her hand, she approached the counter, to the bundle Charlo had placed on the counter. Wrapped in cream padded wrapping paper, bound over and over with brown masking tape. Her name – Captain Harte – in black marker. No postage.

'Thank you,' she said.

'No tick-tock,' he said with a smile. 'I listen, and said to her it was okay.'

'A woman brought it here,' she said. 'Charlo?'

'Yes. A granny woman with long blonde hair. She was not pretty. Fat, very fat. Like my sister, Veronika. Look a little like her, too.'

'Okay... thank you.'

Her eyes fastened on the package, she put a five-dollar bill on his guestbook, and focused on walking along the hall, to the stairs, as though not a single drink had crossed her lips.

She placed the package on the dresser, sat opposite it on the edge of the bed, re-assembling her thoughts.

What the hell is it?

A horse's head. A severed hand. Casey's...

There was only one way to find out.

PART TWO

CHAPTER 31

J enny Elizabeth Casey was born as drunk as her screaming mother at 04:45 in the morning, seconds after sunrise. A newly born hollering in the dawn chorus and intermittent traffic noise. The circus was in town in more ways than one. She learnt these details years later. Her mother, in a sober interlude, imparted them during an act of selfish offloading. It made Jenny finally decide to leave her old life behind. She'd been called after her mother's mother – yet another, 'Little old wine drinker me.' Her father could have been a dwarf, she had heard, from the circus. Mother couldn't be sure. She'd been going through a rough spell at the time with depression and all.

'You'll never know the half of what I had to endure, Jenny.'

For fuck's sake, Jenny had thought. *The stuff you get to hear.*

Next morning, Jenny caught the bus to the recruiting centre in a Midland town and joined the army. Up until her mother's outpourings, she had been considering going full-time in Lidl, working in a distribution centre, and had only applied for the army for the craic. She'd surprised herself at the interview, giving a good account of herself as though she were speaking about another person; fielding questions confidently, knowledgably – and yet she understood there was pressure on the recruiters to recruit more females into the ranks. There were so few looking to sign up. After passing her medical she'd waited for the numbers to reach platoon strength before training commenced. Her mother didn't want her to leave but Jenny'd witnessed too many of her drying-out sessions. She was sick of listening, trying to help, sick of having nonsense funnelled into her ears. That last revelation had squeezed the heart too tightly... A dwarf father. Could have been! Down the years her mother always portrayed Jenny's father as a variation of a big Lotto win – handsome, dark-haired, tall – Marlon Brando, film hunk. Now he was possibly a clown dwarf in a travelling circus. Not that she had anything against dwarves. She'd loved Sleepy in *Snow White*, for crying out loud. Hobbits, too.

Anyway. Here she sat, in a kibbutz, in her aunt's chalet. Gretta had dumped the creepy statue at that officer's hotel. Her aunt worked as a head nurse at the kibbutz hospital and had been living in Israel for 21 years. Kibbutznik, she'd referred to herself as. Some years back her husband, a conscript, had been killed by sniper fire in Lebanon. They had had a baby who died a day short of turning a month old. She'd never remarried, nor had another kid.

Jenny got in touch with Gretta during her first visit to Israel, after crossing the border with Captain Myles O'Rourke's tour group. Biggest mistake of her life was to get sucked into that peddling lark and to make pals with that class eejit Nora Sexton. When she'd confided in Gretta, her aunt's small, tight lips opened and closed several times. Jenny hadn't seen a person stuck so badly for words.

Finally, Gretta said Jenny was heading toward a highly dangerous storm and she wanted to hear nothing more. Advised her sternly not to mention she'd a relative living in Israel.

'Got that? Not my dogfight.'

'Got it, Gretta.'

Dead right about the storm. So when Lukas beat up Nora for stealing two of the small statue things, which she hadn't – it was only one – someone else must have taken the other – she just scarpered with the thing in her knapsack, because that crazy Pole was baying for blood. You could smell the menace from him. Everyone feared him, except his brother Janus. Ugly men who believed they were otherwise. Their mirrors, she'd quipped to Nora, must lie to them so they won't get smashed to smithereens.

After legging it from the nightclub, she'd called Gretta in a state of panic and fear. Gretta gave her a pick-up point and drove to collect her in an old lime-green Volkswagen. She lathered her niece's ear with her tongue for most of the journey back north to Qiryat Shmona.

'Look at you – the state of you – Jesus, Mary... Your mother to a tee. And that is no compliment, Jenny. Whose blood is that you're wearing? Stop your crying. Tell me what the hell is going on with you? What sort of mess are you in? It's that smuggling business, isn't it? That you told me about. I warned you, didn't I? I warned you. Gosh. If a pig blew wind you'd move from it in a hurry, but when your aunt gave you advice, you chose to ignore it... Now, you're snared in the pig's wind – I can bloody well smell it off you, girl...'

Jenny answered her question passively. Informed her she'd told Nora she wanted nothing more to do with the racket. Nora had said not to worry, she would tell O'Rourke, who would notify the Dabrowskis. If she wanted.

Gretta didn't speak for a long time. Jenny said to end the strained silence, 'What else would you expect from the daughter of a clown dwarf? That's who Mam said my dad most likely was, a bloody circus clown.'

Gretta erupted in laughter. 'That was me your dopey ma was on about – he was a lovely man. I went with him for about a year and then he picked up with someone else. He didn't like Maura at all... The way she looked down at him. I mean more than from just a height.'

'Who was my father, then?'

'Only Jesus knows.'

*

Gretta had delayed an hour before journeying home to the kibbutz south-east of Qiryat Shmona, after delivering the package, to be sure she wasn't being followed. She'd removed the blonde wig in a car park and left it in a bin outside a fast-food restaurant. When she'd parked outside her kibbutz home, she joined Jenny on the blanket-covered couch on the veranda and lit a cigarette. Gretta was cold after the adrenalin rush of the drop-off, the long drive, the fear of being found out. The things your family can walk you into, the things you do for people carrying the same blood as you. Gretta wished she'd thought of a plan better than simply abandoning the figurine in that seedy hotel to the Irish officer Jenny had mentioned. But the options narrowed to one. Getting rid of the object would take murderous men off their trail, at least. Or it should.

'Thanks, Gretta. Thanks for helping me out,' Jenny said.

Jackals yipped in the scrubland behind the horseshoe cluster of chalets. Most were new builds and vacant, awaiting occupants. Beyond the scrubland were minefields, braceleted with barbed wire and skull-and-crossbones warning signs; some 20 years old, others 50.

'What are your plans?' Gretta asked, a little jittery, looking at the glowing tip of her cigarette.

'I'm not sure,' Jenny almost whispered, stunned. She thought the plans were sorted. Stay here until the heat cooled and she could think of a way forward.

Gretta's courage must be failing. 'You probably shouldn't desert, you know?'

'I don't think I've got much choice, really.'

'You could have handed yourself over to the Irish officer – it could still be a plan?'

Jenny recalled Nora's last text to her, from a new phone number, about Harte, not to say anything to the cow. She would do her no favours. Stay away from her. The bitch's card was marked.

'Btw wher U? Yeah, Nora. I'm going to tell you. Fat chance. Good job I never told you about Gretta.'

'Tks for dat – will pass on name to lads.'

What sort of a gobshite am I? Giving a clue about Gretta…

Locating the officer's whereabouts had proved easier than expected, Gretta said, intruding on Jenny's thoughts. She'd called into the Jerusalem MP Detachment and got the information from a desk NCO, a Nepalese MP with limited English. A man eager to help, especially when she had the same 'very lovely speak like ma'am.'

Jenny said into a short silence, 'I thought that I could stay here for a while.'

'There's a lot of time and police hours being put into searching for you – that sort of thing costs money. They're not giving up, are they? You're going to have to face the music sometime and once you do, it'll soon be over and you can get on with your life. Then... maybe... we could see about making it possible for you to stay with me. They can always use extra help in the orange groves and in the kitchens, and you can think about furthering your education.'

'I... I suppose,' Jenny said, the words not her thoughts.

'You suppose what, Jenny?'

'I don't want you to get into trouble. But I can't just walk up to them and plead memory loss or something, can I?' And...'

'And?'

'Before this evening, the plan was that I would stay with you for a while until we figured out the best way forward. I didn't want to let the blue statue go – I could have used it to make a deal, you know. Like you see in the movies and that. Leverage, right.'

'The sight of it made my stomach turn. I wanted to be shot of it. That's the one good thing you've done. As for memory loss. Of course, it happens. Amnesia caused by the shock of getting a blow to your head and seeing your friend Nora being kicked about.'

'A new plan, then, Aunt Gretta. But what brought it about?'

'Jenny, your mother and half-brother are in Israel. Along with two Irish detectives. And—'

'She and Willie are here!'

'Yes. Well, in Lebanon. As good as.'

Jenny hadn't seen her mother in four years, Willie in three. She'd broken the connection, though there hadn't been one, not in the real sense. Willie was two years older than her, thin and lanky, with a dimple on his chin. Soft lad, easily hurt. He had a bad stomach since he was little. She'd regretted leaving him behind. Consoled herself by telling herself she'd shown him it was possible to get away from someone who was bringing you down. Lied to herself because Willie would never learn how to let go.

While in bed, the decision to leave for the Jerusalem MP Detachment in the morning sealed in trust and faith with her aunt, Jenny determined to wait for an hour after hearing Gretta's bedroom door close. Only then would she clear off. Gretta's fresh scheme was for Jenny to present herself to the MPs and request she be brought to a hospital. Jenny voiced enough protest so Gretta would not think she'd given in too easily. It worked; she believed she'd gotten through to her.

That was so not happening.

She wrote her aunt a long letter, thanking her for her kindness, how much she regretted taking this course of action, but she simply couldn't face going back. Her thoughts shifted... But where to with no resources? Maybe get in touch with Nora, ask if she could help? Silly thinking, because Nora was the reason she was in bother. This mad idea sparked in her, after reading of the estimated value of the two statues O'Rourke had in his bag.

Over half a million dollars or whatever because of their age, craftsmanship, gems, and their long and spooky history.

The idea? Simple. Take one and flog it at a cut price to speed its sale – Nora said she knew a guy who knew a guy who dealt in antiquities. What, she'd said, dripping scorn, was the muppet O'Rourke going to do about it? Making a couple of hundred bucks for taking a huge risk like they had been doing to date was small fry. Made sense how she said it. But they hadn't known the statues weren't O'Rourke's. They belonged to the Poles.

She eased herself up quietly, took her duffle bag from under the bed. In it were some food items, a couple of beers, a blanket, a map and other bits and pieces. In her jeans pocket she had about 170 dollars and 80 shekels. On the veranda, easing the door shut behind her, she swept in a deep breath. The air was scented with the sweet fragrance of orange trees and dew in the cool night. Stars hung in the clear skies, the thin peel of a moon. She turned the keys to her aunt's lime-green Volkswagen in her hand and went to the car.

CHAPTER 32

The blue idol. Her bedroom guest. She'd woken in the middle of the night with the sensation of hands gripping her throat. She felt their deep squeeze, the shots of pain and of panic. When she opened her eyes she saw a black apparition at the end of her bed. It was as though a mass had sundered from the blackest of clouds. *Christ!* Whatever it was faded to ordinary blackness.

No. No...

She wondered if the sighting had been no more than her overstressed brain acting out a mirage of sorts.

Who had brought the idol to the hotel? And why? She did not think it the same one they had taken from the ambush site – was this possible? She was due to drive across the border this afternoon. Fredericksen and Morris were to brief her on her future. They would discuss the case and meet with Casey's parents or as it had turned out, her mother and half-brother, Willie. The Irish detectives, too, to bring them up to speed – slow speed – on the case. Had Casey deposited it here for her? If not, who? And why? If it were not the one taken from the scene of the shootout, then it must be Casey who delivered the demon relic? It must have been. What other explanation was there? Her eyes studied the piece and she gathered her thoughts.

Its origins are from Ur, formerly one of the oldest Mesopotamian cities, dating from the 4th millennium BC, in southern Iraq. Abraham and his family left there to become desert wanderers, to follow God's voice. Emer pondered if Abraham simply fled to save his children from being sacrificed to a deity. Perhaps he was a priest and had some involvement in those rituals? She had heard someone say that ancient cave drawings were the artist's handshake down the ages – this idol in the same regard was a breath of evil. An indelible mark.

Okay.

Do I bring the relic across the border?

Avi Cohen would have tightened security, for sure. Besides, it was dangerous to bring the idol on any length of journey – she could be followed, ambushed yet again. Who in the military police could she trust? Lahr had fallen in with the Dabrowskis. Who else could have tipped someone off about their trip to Tyre for the handover to the Iraqi museum officials? Fredericksen? Hardly. Morris? No.

She made a call. In the bathroom she stared at the red mark around her throat, like a rash had taken hold there. A welt of evil. *Really? Did I do this to myself?*

CHAPTER 33

Two hours later she sat in Avi Cohen's Jerusalem office, watching the Israeli pour coffee into two beige polystyrene cups. Spectacles perched on his hennaed hair, his belly a little slack around his pale blue shirt. She was feeling somewhat edgy. She'd almost knocked down a pedestrian on the way. Her nerves were strung out and she sucked in deep breaths to stem the tide of nerves threatening to consume her.

'May I?' he said, eyes on the pillowcase on his desk.

'Of course.'

He handed her the coffee and took a sip of his. Cohen removed the idol from the pillowcase and kept it flat on his palm. He moved it up and down as though weighing the object. Pulling his glasses down, he examined the idol close-up, touching the inscription on its back. Then he slipped it back into the pillowcase and went and washed his hands.

'It's not the same as the one I saw in the photographs you showed me last time you were here.'

'I thought so,' she said. 'Why have you brought it to me?'

'I think you know why. Have you heard what happened on the way to Tyre – you know about Lahr?' He said. 'Yes, I heard. Most unfortunate, indeed. Let us talk about all of that... but...' He nodded and seemed to dislodge a frown that crossed like a deep trench across his forehead. 'Tell me...' he said, pointing.

'Oh, it's a rash – I must have, I don't know, come into contact with something, with my hands and...' She shrugged and continued, 'Stress. I was there. I saw Lahr being shot. I saw who shot him. I shot the men who had fired at us.'

'And how are you coping with those events?'

She did not say fine as both knew it would be a lie. She felt a little guilty about shooting Boland and Dabrowski, in spite of telling herself she shouldn't feel even half of a pinch of remorse. If anything there should be anger and self-reproach for not having done the job properly.

She said, 'I've got a mountain of stuff on my plate right now; let's just leave it at that.'

Cohen made a call in Hebrew and when finished he said, 'I have sent for the people, my son, at the Israel Museum to take this away. But you haven't answered my question. I don't fully know why you have brought this to me.'

'Would I have made it across the border?' she asked, growing a small smile.

'There was that possibility. Slight. You and your vehicle would have been thoroughly searched at the crossing – no doubt – but would you have made it as far as there for such a search to happen?'

'You said "good" at our first meeting, when I answered your question about the UN acting against the Dabrowski brothers and others – at the time I said no.'

'We have people of ours that we need to clear out from that crossing. We are not too certain about who they are and how many of them there are – when we do move, we will cut at the roots. Ours and yours.'

'So is it better I bring that thing with me or leave it here?'

'You have made a good decision. One that has most likely saved your life.'

She said, 'Anything on Casey?'

'There is some news. We visited the kibbutz where she had been staying with her aunt – the woman reported her car as missing and that her niece had taken it. We found the car. Casey left a note to say where it could be found, on the seafront in Akko. She's slipped from our radar, but at least we can now presume she's alive.'

Emer sipped at her coffee. She added two sachets of brown sugar and stirred with a plastic spoon. This would be positive news to bring her family, and leading information for the two detectives. It pissed her off, though, for such information to come from Avi. Had Myles O'Rourke, Captain Antique Advice himself, known any of this? Had Sexton, the others? Of her aunt? It's like a brother in Ireland sending a message to another brother in America to pass it on to another brother living in Ireland. Happened to her ex.

'He is a good man, this Lahr, I think?' Avi said.

'Yes, from what I know of him – he seems a decent sort. A real family man.'

'I think you like him.'

She said nothing.

'Will you stick to the truth?' Cohen said.

'I have done so far. He needed the money for—'

'He was implicated. I thought so.'

'Sadly, yes.'

'You are not sure if his implication will be revealed in the report, or if you want to write it in, to begin with?

'Yes, I don't know where I'm at. I also suspect a deal will be done with Boland, depending on what he has to offer. He would have to say a lot of significant things. Or else give an undertaking not to. He's the weakest link so they'll tweak him this way and that to suit.'

'Hmm,' Cohen mulled, 'and Lahr had mitigating circumstances, had he not, for turning himself inside out.'

'His daughter – you knew?'

The silence lingered until she realised he was not going to tell her. She formed the notion that he held every card in the deck.

She said, 'Right now, I want to get back home and get on with living my life.'

'If I can help you steer a way through the mess. Ring me. Be sure that you do.'

'Ring you?'

His eyes brought hers to the covered idol. 'One good turn deserves another. At least, we have one of these in our custody. There will be no gathering of the six. Emer, you are aware that this meeting never happened, that you never gave me this instrument of evil. The very second that you are gone from this office, this conversation about the Ur artefact never happened.'

She'd no intention of blabbing what she'd done to anyone. She hoped Cohen wasn't going to sell the idol, that he was a man of his word. Trust? She supposed it was going to take her a hell of a long time to give it to anyone.

He said, 'Be mindful. Someone believes this is in your possession, and suspicion alone often brings uninvited attention. So be cautious.'

'Yes.'

He went to the window and peered through the glass. 'My people are here.' Meaning it was time for her to leave. He wrote a number on the back of his business card and gave it to her. Glanced at the wall clock.

She would drop into the detachment to see Pedney, to ask him something, and to see if they needed anything brought to Headquarters. Time to spare but she was in no rush to spend it.

CHAPTER 34

Pedney, as it turned out, was due to arrive back at base tomorrow, and he was delighted to be leaving 'prison.'

'They put me to Nepbatt… It is good…'

She knew the reason so didn't ask.

They drank herbal tea, lime and ginger. He was alone, again manning the desk. When she asked where the others were, he said, his eyes cast downwards, that Chief Joseph and Staff Benny were on patrol.

'Will I get them on radio for you, Captain?' he said.

'No… but you need to answer my question. I saw Chief Joseph behaving very angrily towards you a while back. I saw him…' She gestured with her forefinger and put on a cross face.

'Chief Joseph?' he said, a frown creasing his clear forehead. 'He always angry.' He gave a long and slow nod. 'He just say that I should not say anything about finding the devil, that it was Jerusalem MP business, not SIS.'

'I see.'

'Chief Joseph is always the angry man. Staff Sergeant Benny, too – he say I the most stupid person.'

Always the angry man? she thought. Nothing like what she had seen of the Fijian. A real chief, as Benny had said of him. And a kava farmer back home. Charismatic, tall and muscular, easy to imagine his being an intimidating presence; his geniality buffed the rough edges. Or camouflaged it? Reproached Pedney instead of complimenting him on his find. Why? Sounded as though he'd wanted to hog the glory for himself. Pedney was always being frowned upon and for him to make the discovery... Well, did the Chief and Benny take that as a slight? A sour joke that Pedney with all his perviness, his low-grade police skills, had found an item steering the missing person case down a smuggling route. A potentially murderous one, too, as it soon turned out.

'Irish woman, she find you?' he said.

'Irish woman?'

'She say she want to speak with you. Old lady, very nice.'

Journalist, she thought. *Or Casey's aunt, most likely.*

She left the detachment after warning Pedney to say nothing of her visit. There was another reason why Chief Joseph and Benny had been angry toward Pedney. Inadvertently, he'd screwed them over.

CHAPTER 35

Cohen's phone sounded as he entered his office. While loosening his wine-coloured tie, he listened to his lead operative's report about the happenings on the Lebanese coastal road to Tyre.

The Irish officer. He liked this young woman very much. Of course, she was far too young for him and he doubted whether the appeal ran in both directions. One can hope, though. And one can try. The world turns on the rendering of favours, does it not?

She survived. Her companion too. Hmm.

We are cut from the same cloth, she and I.

He understood the Irish woman would search for the information she needed and indeed he would help her with any assistance she requested. Up to a point. Cohen disconnected and pocketed his phone, rolled up his tie and put it in his drawer, next to his service pistol and clips of 9mm rounds. Leaning back in his computer chair, he swivelled toward the air conditioning to savour its cool breeze. He wore a light blue shirt, the underarms dark with perspiration, and a pair of navy slacks beginning to get too tight for him.

Too much of the good life, he thought, undoing the waist button. He smoothed his hair, a little oily from the fresh haircut. Stroked his moustache. His thoughts switched to Baghdad, where he had worked as a ground operative for several years, spying for the government, reporting on the disintegration of the Hussein regime, the exact locations of ammunition depots, airfields, the likely storage places for weapons of mass destruction, the usual haunts visited by persons of interest, their routines, hobbies, vices, weak points. Many vices, many of those people.

He dealt in antiques in the souk, fake and genuine, and sold little but enough not to have anyone wondering how he managed to remain in business. Spoke Arabic with a Yemeni flourish, the language of his parents. His background had withstood vetting by the Republican Guard. His dinar and dollars, easy charm, and rare whiskey loosened padlocked tongues. Twice, during his spell there, he had to feed the Tigris waters with the bodies of men who'd nursed doubts about the hennaed-haired stranger who said he was from Aden, using that word to describe Yemen.

Into his shop one late afternoon, an old Kurdish man arrived... He waited for a browser to leave before approaching the counter. He said he was from the northern city of Kirkuk and had something of interest to show him. He had a willing buyer already but if he were to offer a better price...

Instantly, Avi recognised what had been placed on his glass-topped counter. An idol of Ur. He picked it up, ran the piece under a magnified eye, the tip of his finger along an engraved symbol.

'Where did you acquire this?' Avi queried.

The answer was a hard-eyed leonine stare.

'Do you know what it is?' Avi said.

'Yes.'

'How much do you want?'

'One hundred thousand US dollars.'

Avi whistled. Worth more, worth less, depending on the seller's circumstances. These were not good; Avi knew from experience. For the elderly man was the cut of sheer desperation.

'If you are found with this in your possession...' Avi said, having no need to complete the sentence.

The man reached for the figurine but Avi gripped his wrist, like a handcuff.

'I have 30,000 dollars here. That is all. In cash. US dollars.'

The Kurd sighed, rubbed his lips, his expression that of a hungry man having to devour something far from appetising. His nod weak, resigned.

In the following days, Avi noticed unusual activities in the souk, became aware of being followed. From years spent in the field of following people, of hunting, of being a ghost, Avi had no doubts. Who had the Kurd gone to before him to sell the piece? This had to be the link. He trusted his own paranoia, became spooked enough to have his handler call him in, and arrived back in Tel Aviv later, with the idol in his suitcase.

Two down; four to go, he had thought. Three now, thanks to the Irish officer with the name Emer.

CHAPTER 36

In old Akko, she visited the vaulted dining hall built by the Crusaders and then descended some steps to a lighted walkway along a labyrinth of tunnels. Routes the knights used to escape to their vessels after Saladin's forces breached the city's walls in 1291. Jenny read about it in a brochure she'd picked up at the Century Youth Hostel, situated just before a short lead into a rabbit warren of alleyways. She went there after spending one night in a pricey hotel room – the sink stained with streaks of the purple dye she'd used to colour her short hair. She wore silver studs in her ear lobes and a silver ring with a blue gemstone on a little finger she could never straighten after a fall from a playground swing. Rosewood prayer beads around her neck, with a blue meru. Jenny hoped she was taking the soldier look from herself by implementing such changes. Some of the clothes she had put in the waste-bin, she later saw on the backs of a couple of hostel residents. In particular, her army T-shirt bearing her name. She went to approach the young woman to warn her but the moment was lost, when she climbed into a taxi.

Jenny had come to the old part of the city, knowing that UN personnel rarely went there, preferring to drive straight on to Haifa, Tel Aviv, and Jerusalem. She shared a dorm with a few others and mostly kept to herself. Though this wasn't always possible, as some guys imagined her being alone as an open invitation to try it on. She said she was waiting for her girlfriend to fly in from Athens. More or less informing them of her lezzie status. Which she half was, she'd told herself. So no lie.

She wandered the warren on the afternoon of the fifth day since abandoning Aunt Gretta's Volkswagen. Nursing a cold smoothie, she stopped to listen to a guide giving a party of tourists some of the port's history – the Crusaders, Marco Polo and other stuff she had already read about. She tried to pay enough attention to take her mind off more pressing matters. Her money wouldn't last forever. Then what? There had to be an end play to the game, yeah?

There he is, again. She had spotted him earlier.

He looked like an Irish traveller or at a push even a Roma gypsy. Foxy hair, thick foxy eyebrows, freckles. Firebeard. She'd been drawn to his Irishness, fretted he could be UN. But he was local; she could tell from the way he interacted with others.

She lowered her head, avoiding eye contact, quickening her pace, leaving the tourists behind.

'Hello, hello,' he said.

She'd to pull up short when he stood in front of her. He was of average height and build, his eyes as green as moistened mint leaves. His smile revealed a curve of white teeth.

'I see you here each day – you would like a guide, yes. I can show you everyplace.'

'No, thanks.'

'Sorry, sorry, my name is Salah. What is yours?'

'Teresa,' she lied.

'Please allow me to buy you a coffee.'

She looked at her smoothie. It had lost is flavour and its chill. A coffee sounded good. She could learn something from him; he might know of a place where she could work under the radar, waitressing or bar work.

He indicated a table for three outside a café. Public enough, if he were to try anything on. She could scream... Boy, could she scream. Three things she did well – scream, run, and climb like a monkey.

An oil cloth of medieval sailing vessels, azure skies and a burning castle on the shoreline covered the table. There were six cushioned chairs with rattan backs. A coffee stand displayed pastries bothered by flies. Curtains of different coloured strips seemed to screen off a kitchen, which she made out when a woman came through to serve them. He spoke to her in Arabic and she returned to the kitchen, quicker than when she had emerged.

'Arabic coffee, I ordered this for us. Nam?' he said, when they were seated.

'Nam.'

'Ah, so you speak Arabic.'

'A few words, that's all.'

While he fished a packet of Lucky Strikes from his shirt pocket, he asked if she smoked. Reached, his questioning eyes on her, for the red lighter resting on the image of the tablecloth's burning castle.

She accepted his cigarette, watched the flame on the lighter glowing as a fiery tear.

A straggle line of tourists went by, chattering in German.

'Do you like Akko?' he said, staring at the backs of the last of them to pass by.

'Yes, it's nice – do you live here?'

'Sometimes.'

'I see.'

'Where are you from?' he asked. 'You're not English... Maybe Irish?'

'Yes. Irish.'

He moved his head one way then the other, narrowed his eyes as he appraised her through the mist of two tobacco clouds, his and hers.

She smiled nervously, touched her throat.

'Do you know,' he breathed, 'Miss Jenny, that you are in most serious trouble.'

There wasn't even time for her scream to leave her throat.

CHAPTER 37

She was tired of being in this office of Fredericksen's. He'd applied more 'x's to the calendar dates and the blades of the ceiling fan seemed to creak louder than before.

Morris spoke in a rush. 'Sexton is being repatriated tomorrow. She's refused to engage with the detectives, even after they'd leaned heavily on her. Quartermaster Boland had his lower left arm amputated and it's expected he'll follow Sexton as soon as possible. We can deal with Sexton and Boland on our own turf. Timo – Lahr, is still in an induced coma. His family is coming out to see him.'

He hesitated and then said, 'Lukas Dabrowski isn't expected to see through the night.'

She felt nothing at hearing this, unless numbness was a feeling.

Shouldn't I feel something? No, they tried to kill me. Keep telling yourself that – never stop telling yourself! Would you prefer to be the one wrapped in plastic, like G.I.'s mother in the furze?

Fredericksen said, 'I'm assigning you as officer in charge of the SIS and I have asked...' He deferred to Morris with a hand gesture.

Morris continued, 'It's a yearlong position.'

'A year... A year!' she said, incredulous. 'I was looking forward to getting home tomorrow or sooner...'

Fredericksen smiled. Morris scratched his chin, at an angry mossie bite fresh from the evening before.

He said, 'I want you to think about it... You can go home with the first rotation in October and come out two weeks later with the last. It won't be classified as leave.'

She said nothing, not to even say she would think about it, that she would at least bring the proposal – order – that far. Her thoughts were on other matters. This couldn't be all about what they wanted or expected of her.

'I want to interview Boland,' she said crisply. 'I want to see him eye to eye. I'd include Janus Dabrowski, too, but that wouldn't be a good idea now that his brother's about to die.'

The men glanced at each other.

Morris said grudgingly, 'Okay, interview Boland. The detectives said he's been involved in criminality back home for a long time – we've to decide if he's going to be court-martialled or wrung through the civilian court system.'

'As long as he is charged with attempted murder,' Emer said, 'and as an accomplice to murder, I don't care what court he's in.'

Fredericksen eased in what he had to say off the back of a mild cough. 'Talk to him, but not alone and make a recording – and don't exceed his doctor's advice about the time you can spend with his patient.'

He was asserting his authority over her to Morris, who tried to keep his expression neutral but failed.

'One more thing,' Emer said, a little surprised that she was the one to raise it. 'The idol – is there any update on the circumstances of how it went missing?'

'No,' Fredericksen said. 'I spoke to the men who'd been on checkpoint and recorded statements. Either they are responsible for the theft...or the idol was not in your Landcruiser to begin with.'

What he had said bounced off the insides of her skull like a rubber ball; then it stopped moving to pinch at a nerve. 'Are you saying Lahr and I stole it? What the hell did you think we were going to hand over to the Iraqis in Tyre? Marshmallows?'

Fredericksen leaned back his chair, as though the words had punched him in the chest. Morris chuckled. Apologetically,

155

Fredericksen said, 'As police officers we have to consider every possibility and everyone in those possibilities – I'm sorry – and don't speak in such a disrespectful tone to your commanding officer again.'

'Why not? What you'll do? Send me home.'

'Captain Harte,' Morris said, 'we still have a missing soldier to find.'

'And I thought the super cops were here for that purpose?'

'She's military – she could be missing for a long time – and you know the Guards won't be here for more than a week or two. She's one of ours, good or bad.'

Her eyes backed off from Fredericksen. She told them briefly what she had learned from Avi Cohen about Casey and her Aunt Gretta. Sightings of her – solid info that she's alive. 'Good,' Morris said. 'We learned of the sister from Casey's mother, but she didn't know of her whereabouts in Israel, or even if her sister was still in the country.' Fredericksen said, 'You organise the meeting between Casey's mother and aunt, Gerry, yes?' Turning to Emer, he continued, 'Let me know what you need in the section.'

'I haven't decided if I'm staying,' she said.

Morris said evenly, 'Lend it some thought.'

If she chose to ship home she would face being back into routine barrack duties, probably in charge of training raw recruits? *Do I want that? There are better crosses to nail myself to.*

Once the media got wind of the shootout, they would badger her for interviews and whatnot. Haunt the hell out of her.

I need a drink and maybe a chill pill.

There was a tall and thin young man waiting for her outside. He was wearing green chinos and a light blue shirt.

'Are you Captain Harte?' he asked. 'The Duty Room NCO said you were at a meeting.'

Emer nodded slightly, as though reluctantly owning up to her name.

'Can I have a word with you?' he said.

'Who are you?' she said.

'Sergeant Harris, David.'

Oh, she thought. *Sexton's husband.*

And he's here, why? To heckle me about the circumstances behind his wife slitting her wrist?

'I see,' she said, indicating the MP Club. At this hour they could sit outside without being disturbed.

He was smoking when she returned to their table with two colas. A nervous sort, Nora and a heart tattooed on his left forearm.

The poor fucker.

'So, what can I do for you?' she said, untabbing her can.

He drew on his cigarette. His knee was bobbing up and down. Out to the sea, the horizon nursed a cruise ship.

He could not look her straight in the eye when he asked, 'I want to know what you're doing about the bastard who beat my wife up. How much progress have you made?'

She sipped at her cola, enjoyed its flow down her throat. He looked at the face of his cigarette.

'What has Nora told you?' she asked.

'Nothing. She says she can't remember a bloody thing – one second she's with your one, Jenny, and the next she's lying on her back in hospital. That's as much as she's given me.'

'Have you spoken to her doctor?'

'Yes.'

'And?'

'She's in a bit of bother, from what he said, physically and mentally, and I get that, you know, but...'

She let the silence grow into what he said next.

'No one is telling me anything. I spoke with some of the others on the tour and none of them.' He shrugged. 'It's like, I don't know, they're all hiding something... Are they?'

'You know I'm not at liberty to discuss the case with you, not at this point,' she said.

'Then I heard on the street about the smuggling. Was Nora involved in that?'

She sighed and said, 'David... I'm off the back of a murder attempt on my life, a comrade of mine is in a coma... I'm not sure where I'm at with the case at the minute.'

He took a slow pull on his cigarette, tempting her into loosening the cellophane on a cigar and helping herself to his lighter. She caved.

'I'm sorry,' he said, 'it's just that no one is able to cast any light on what happened and they don't want to talk about it – and – you know – no one has asked me how she's doing or offered to help in any way. Your man O'Rourke, the tour officer in charge, he's a sop. Said it was just one of those things that happens to people every so often... and shrugged.' He paused and added, 'Do you think one of our own gave her the hiding? Is that why I'm up against a wall of silence?'

She said through the bluish grey of cigar and cigarette smoke, 'I think your answers lie with Nora. And I'd give her a little time before you push her for them.'

'Is she going to be charged?'

'For the drug use – she'll probably be discharged. The army has a zero tolerance on that; you're aware of its policy. Her comrades have all been tested for illicit substances too.'

'Jesus,' he said, scratching his earlobe. 'If she's given her ticket, we won't be able to pay the mortgage.'

What do I say to that? she thought. *He has concerns he knows nothing about. His wife's cheating on him with two men, her miscarriage... He seems a good bloke; what other women would describe as a 'keeper.'*

'Her doctor told me that you were the last person to see her before she tried to take her own life,' he said evenly. 'So what exactly did you say to her?'

'I asked her some questions.'

He nodded his head twice, then looked off into the distance as though to rein in thoughts that were in danger of getting too far from him.

He turned and looked straight at Emer. 'And a consequence of what you asked, she did that, ma'am? You'd no right to quiz her when she was under medical supervision.'

'I had every right.'

She stood and told him that if she acquired news about his wife's assailant, she would be in touch – and likewise, she said, knowing it would never happen, if Nora ever remembered anything... he might reciprocate.

CHAPTER 38

In a darkened room, a chink of light showing between blackout curtains, Jenny wriggled her fingers. The cable restraints pinched her wrists. Still groggy, she tried to determine her location, her options. There were none. She was tightly bound to a hardback kitchen chair; ties at the ankles, around her wrists pinned behind her back, her arms bound by rope across her chest, so tight it dug into her shoulders and breasts. She needed to pee and the cloth that filled her mouth muffled her cry and tasted of wood shavings. Some fluff caught in her throat and she coughed up bits of vomit. The world tasted sour. Jenny focused her eyes on the ray of light. She was sitting sideways to a long and narrow window, the beam of light a narrow dust-moted channel of what? Hope? She pieced together aspects of her abduction: the heavy-handed throw and grab of Salah and his partner's hands, their hurling her into the kitchen – Salah's hands fiercely compressing her throat, the other's eyes scratching wildly at the back of her skull. Dragged up a flight of tiled stairs to this room – this room? Then beat into submission with kicks and blows she did not see coming in the darkness.

She felt sore all over. As the shock was wearing off, she began very much to feel the cuts, the knocks, his hard squeeze to her throat. So many pains came to her at once, ebbing to a single source, so they could be counted as one. A tear fell, and another. Their slide meandered along her swollen cheek, ending in their saltiness burning her cut upper lip. Footsteps.

Approaching.

She felt and smelt the sweet flow of pee... She could not contain her fear.

CHAPTER 39

Of the day she remembered a waning moon in a clear blue sky, and the hours running into the horrors of discovery. Where a woman's body was discovered in the furze, where a child's hope and beliefs were incalculably shattered, resulting in her wishing for many years not to have been the discoverer, the one who ended G.I.'s hopes and beliefs. During her 18-month cadetship training on the Curragh Camp, she'd encountered three strange things she'd never seen in her earlier time: a long-tailed sheep, a beautifully coloured macaw perched on a woman's shoulder, and a mad bull, which escaped from a nearby abattoir, that she was tasked to put out of its misery. A clear shot through the bull's forehead ended its torment. The officer in charge of the detail thought she would refuse to squeeze the trigger – he'd asked for a volunteer and then detailed someone who hadn't stepped forward. Saint Brigid's plains they may well be, but she didn't intend to plant her feet on its short grass anytime soon... so she crumpled the invitation to her cadet class reunion in the officers' mess, with its panoramic window view of the rolling grassland. She threw the card into the wire basket beside her desk and hauled her attention to where it was most needed.

Emer opened the bulging wallet folder containing the investigation file. The case notes needed updating, statements typing, but she wasn't yet able to focus properly. Report writing could wait for a while longer. Case notes were different. These needed doing; these were waymarks, thoughts, and facts – these she could not ignore for too long.

She opened her mail. Nothings, requests for photocopies of old files. The last one she opened, was from the Transport NCO, who was now on leave.

Ma'am,

Please find documentation attached, you asked for...

Frances.

Emer read and reread, picking out the bones. Chief Joseph and Benny were in Lebanon on the day of the attack.

They crossed at Metula Border Point.

Emer stared at their registration number.

Metula Border Crossing lay to the north and was not as commonly used as a crossover point as Roshaniqra, which was a little over six kilometres from her billet. It made no sense for Jerusalem military police to use Metula crossing to enter Lebanon. An unnecessary loop of a journey to undertake; 120km longer, at least. So, why travel that route? Obvious.

Who would imagine that military police would cross the border to deal death to two of their own? Military police went to and from Israel and Lebanon frequently – Metula was used by Chief Joseph and Benny because it avoided having to go near UN Headquarters, greatly lessening the chances of their being noticed. Who would bother to check?

Lahr? Me?

We were *both* supposed to be dead.

They were there to receive the idol from Dabrowski and spirit it and themselves back into Israel.

Emer took a can of 7Up from the fridge, untabbed it and slugged hard, the ring momentarily snagging her cold sore. After reapplying creamy ointment to her lip, she pulled her notebook from her cargo pocket to write down some questions for Boland. She knew that he would most likely ignore them. Even so, his silence would be telling. It'd raise more questions for him to answer in court.

Questioning him wasn't absolutely necessary for her to do – but she believed it important to face the man who'd tried to murder her. She wanted to leave no doubt in his mind that she was not afraid of him. She'd quite literally shot one of his arms away, and her bullets had brought a slow death to his obnoxious pal, Lukas Dabrowski.

One fatality, one permanently disabled, another whose fate was currently being determined. She the only one to walk away unscathed. Physically, that was. She'd wept tears for Lahr, for his daughter, and she was angry on his behalf and toward him, and there were periods when her anger would flare up in a volcanic rush.

Was there a point where she could have saved him if she'd acted sooner? No. The action had happened too quickly and in a sort of hazy surrealism. In the days following the killing, she sometimes allowed herself to imagine a different ending – pictured herself and Lahr surviving the clash and the two others turning cold under the Lebanese sun. Birds plucking at their eyes. *If I had kids, a husband, if... Would these scum hurt them to get at me?*

Hannah sprang to mind; her poor, gormless sister.

Call her.

Tomorrow.

CHAPTER 40

L ahr seemed at peace in his hospital bed. She drew a chair close to him and said nothing – asked herself what she was doing here, at the bedside of a man who'd almost gotten her killed.

'Lahr,' she whispered, touching his forearm, 'what the hell were you playing at? Why didn't you tell me beforehand? Jesus. You almost got us both killed. You need to be waking up now – you've got a daughter who needs you. Your family are on their way to see you. That's good, yeah? You'd want to be giving yourself a stir there, because I want to redden your ears... I'll box them off you for being so stupid. Well, one of them.'

Silence.

'I'll call in later.'

On another floor, she waited in a corridor, composing herself. Quartermaster Hughie Boland was in Sexton's former room. She breathed deeply in and out. Fixed her smile and entered the room. She saw the temper flash to his eyes and colour flame his cheeks and throat. His arm arrested at the elbow in a wad of bandages.

I did that.

'What the fuck do you want?' he said, his tone one of whining aggression. 'Haven't you taken enough already?'

'I thought you were expecting me – you look surprised, Boland.'

'I was told to expect an MP, not you. A scummy rat.'

She cautioned him, telling him that whatever he said could be used in evidence.

'I'm not talking to you,' he spat. 'Doctor, Nurse... Get her away from here!' His flexed forearm animated the tattoo of a blue mermaid. 'Look. Look!' he shouted, bringing her eyes to where his other arm used to be.

Emer did not flinch. 'Quartermaster Boland, why did you shoot at me?'

He didn't answer.

'Why did you stop my vehicle on the day in question?'

Silently, his eyes and lips insulted her.

'Why won't you answer my questions?'

No response.

She said, 'Can you explain how you came to have a Luger pistol in your possession?'

His chin went low. But his eyes were still hard, still misty, still full of bad intent.

'Was it because you believed the pistol and its rounds wouldn't be traceable?'

Silence.

'How well did you know the recently deceased Lukas Dabrowski?'

Silence.

'Was he your partner in this crime or your employer? Were you frightened of him?'

He brought up his hand, made a fist.

A threat.

'I'll see you in court,' she said quietly, 'before you go down for 10 years at least... More, if you're found guilty of murder.'

'You know nothing. I won't spend a day in prison.'

'You think you'll cut a deal; I thought as much. Ever ready to rat – but do you know what? You're in a Polish-run hospital, and I saw no one guarding your door. The boss, Janus Dabrowski, yeah... He might want to hear about your deal.'

His worried look broke into the silence...

'Seeing you this worried will make my day for a week.'

'Fuck you.'

'Go on,' she said, the door open, 'give us a wave with your right, oops... left hand.'

'You callous fucking bitch!'

His roar hopped against the slamming door.

Jesus, the callous calling someone else callous – she could only smirk and shake her head at his train of thought.

CHAPTER 41

Shadows darker than shadows. The door closed with a soft click behind them. A dog barked, a car horn sounded, and then the silence seemed to funnel into Jenny's ears. Flowing cold. An image of a blowy day at home came to mind. She was little, out in the back garden, having just put flowers on her dog's grave. She'd loved Mossy and he had been knocked down by the milkman and his stupid van. She'd wanted to dig Mossy up to see if he was alive, because she had said a dozen prayers for him not to be dead. After all, hadn't Father O'Connor said they'd only to ask Jesus for whatever they wanted and they would get it? The trick, he said, was to really believe... Really, really believe in what you wanted. A flick of switch, an unshaded light bulb glowed like a miniature hot sun – momentarily dazzling her until she averted her eyes. Every fibre in her tensed, tried to diminish her being, the natural shrinking action of a small animal about to be pulped to death. For moments she saw the pale yellowy floor tiles, the footwear of the men. Brown trainers with black stripes, tan canvas shoes.

She looked up, painfully aware that one eye of hers was half-closed.

Ginger man and another who was taller than him, bulkier – Fijian. She had seen him before, a couple of times, back at the UN base in south Lebanon and once in Jerusalem at the Zamba Night Club. He'd spoken with Myles O'Rourke and the Dabrowski brothers for a short while and then left.

The ginger man slouched into a dirty and sagging armchair in the corner and crossed his legs, declaring chewing gum stuck between the ridge of his trainer.

'Salah,' the Fijian said, 'thanks… Now give me some time alone with her.'

He got to his feet slowly, sullenly and left.

Jenny wished for a blindfold. A blindfold would mean that they had not made up their minds to kill her.

CHAPTER 42

E mer arrived at the Special Investigation Offices early morning. She sat at Lahr's desk in the large, partitioned office. There was a stillness and a coolness to the air that seemed to put a gentle breeze to the sail of her spirit. Sleep had evaded her for most of the night. She had touched herself and enjoyed it and afterwards felt a little guilty at the intensity of her pleasure. She came in a rush – thinking of a man she had once seen in a hospital, a handsome doctor with a silvery grey beard. A man to whom she had never spoken.

It was not in her to engage in one-night stands, to use a man for sex, to allow herself to be used. She needed to experience a connection with a man, before she could surrender herself. John and one other. That's a dick list, as she'd heard female officers call them. Hers made for quick tallying.

She took the keys to the desk drawers from the rack on the wall, intending to open each to search for any personals of Lahr that should be given to his family. She found nothing of that nature. Three files possibly requiring further investigating: an allegation of child sexual abuse made against an Irish soldier, a historical case; a suicide not proven as such; and lastly, something that made her sit up – a file containing cuttings of the missing idols of Ur, pictures showing frontal, side-on, and rear images. Magnified takes of the cuneiform patterns. The etchings on their backs had geometric shapes of the sort she had seen on stones in museums and at sites like Tara back home. Newspaper articles, too, furnished details about the origins – stuff she already knew. What had made her sit up were not those, but money contained in a small, padded, brown envelope. She counted 15,000 US dollars in 100-dollar bills, and then paused to take a breath. There was more... She finished her counting just as the first trills of birdsong broke loose.

Emer locked the drawer, and with energy drawn from her reserves, she moved the furniture to suit what she thought an investigation office layout should reflect. Not just to make it hers, but also to change the energy, feng shui. She would get in some plants. Harmonise. Distractions. She remembered her marmalade cat, Charm; every time she scolded him for killing a mouse or climbing onto something he shouldn't, he would start to preen himself. It was funny. *Why not take a comb to my hair whenever Morris or Fredericksen bother me?*

Outside, she lit a cigar, could hear the sounds of the camp now in full life, watched a patch of blue sky snared between cloud tumuli. She exhaled a circle of smoke.

The money, Lahr. What the hell, like?

Why the surprise? What did you think? That he was stealing for free? He was the good thief on the Cross? Robin Hood? Cop on.

Robin Hood, in a way. Stealing to help save his daughter's life or prolong it. Why leave money in his desk drawer and not in the section's safe? Where did he get that amount of cash?

A thought landed like a stone hitting a pond.

For me... Was I meant to find it? A bribe of sorts? His desk, now mine? Or what, what else? What other reason? A parting gift for unwitting assistance. My share... Mine?

*

Late afternoon she introduced herself to the five new investigators and briefed them on the cases in progress, fielding questions and assigning investigations to each. Next, she crossed the way to another meeting, this time with Fredericksen, Morris, and the two Irish detectives. With them were Jenny Casey's mother and half-brother, Willie. They sat in the company's operational room. Wall maps of the entire Levant, separate ones of Lebanon and Israel, and another of the globe covered the walls, along with a whiteboard reflecting the current operational activity. NTR written beside each battalion of different international peacekeeping battalions – *Nothing To Report.* She would beg to differ. Peacekeeping. Not peace enforcing. Can a peace ever be truly enforced? Yes. But only if one pulverises a country's people into submission. Or when the sides at odds with each other reached the conclusion that Mother Earth had drank enough blood. The United Nations had neither the means nor, truth be told, the inclination to take on the warmongers.

Casey's mother appeared as though she wasn't long off the back of a heroin addiction, while her son didn't seem as though he was playing with a full pack. Fredericksen commenced proceedings, introducing each in turn to the group. In essence, the lead Irish detective said they'd been liaising with the Israeli police officer in charge of the case, and that although they had found her aunt's car, and CCTV footage of Jenny at several places in the old sector of Akko, the leads and house-to-house follow-up enquiries hadn't yielded any information. Perhaps she'd been spooked and fled the city?

The detectives and her relatives were flying home tomorrow, with the responsibility for the investigation returning to the UN. Emer learned that the two sisters hadn't been reunited: Aunt Gretta declined outright to meet with her elder sibling, citing that she'd brought merely misery to her life while they were growing up, and now her daughter had done likewise. No more.

Emer made a mental note to visit this Aunt Gretta.

It surprised her to see no spark, no energy in either Mrs Casey or her son. Just a docile acceptance of what they'd been told. Why did they bother coming out here? They'd asked no questions at the meeting. Not one. Casey's brother just sat silently with the heat rash strong on his chubby, blank face. Her mother requested only that they never give up looking for her daughter. Please do that much for her.

Emer's attention rambled elsewhere throughout the meeting, trying to decide what she should do about the money. She reckoned it was a bribe... Had to be – for what, though? A bribe, yes. For sure...

A large one, too.

Was it Lahr's intention to cut me in after the fact, buy my silence in the hope I considered his daughter's dire situation – and his – and go along with his scheme?

She said nothing of this to the civilian detectives who'd recorded her statement for their case against Boland. They would be in touch, they said.

Back in her office she photographed the desk, the money, and other documents. Her coffee went cold. Moments beforehand she'd called the team from reviewing their cases and tasked them with bringing the drug dogs and their handlers to conduct searches in Pollog and Camp Tara. Collective punishment, yes. She wanted to build resentment toward Dabrowski and Boland within their respective camps. They, not Harte, had caused these disruptions to their comrades' routine. She was sending a clear message: she wouldn't be intimidated. Before she was through, they'd be sick to the backbone from seeing MPs in their faces.

She dropped in to see Fredericksen, unsure if she would tell him about the money. Her instinct was to protect Lahr and this bothered her. She wasn't like that normally – he had done wrong. Justice was necessary, even allowing for mitigating circumstances.

She said, 'I spoke with Pedney about what Chief Joseph had said to him in the detachment – basically he took issue with him about bringing the idol he found to our attention and not Benny's. And...'

Silence dug its roots deep.

'And, go on?'

'I have proof that Chief Joseph and Benny were in Lebanon on the day of the shooting. I believe they crossed the border to take delivery of the idol – that it was to be a smooth handover but something went wrong. I'm what went wrong.'

'I... We have much to think about,' he said, shaking his head.

Envisioning the loss of a golf date, her thoughts bannered.

'I think we should bring them in for questioning,' Emer said, putting a shot.

'Let me think on things for a while, and I'll get back to you.'

Which wasn't the response she'd wanted to hear. Not a man for making a swift decision, which could sometimes be a weakness. Then, a person who makes the occasional rash decision – as in his intended press release – has to always question himself before he cuts to the chase of what needs doing.

CHAPTER 43

His hand held her forehead firm and steady while the other removed the rag from her mouth.

'Scream and it goes back in deeper,' the Fijian said icily. He cast the cloth aside and rubbed his hands together in a cleansing motion.

'Where am I?' Jenny asked hoarsely, lisping through her bruised and swollen lips. Salah's absence had taken some of the menacing atmosphere from the room. An underlying notion was that she was kidding herself. This man called the shots, and if someone as violent as Salah gave way to him... it said something. Fear stabbed her in the pit of her stomach; her ribs seemed to shrink and squeeze tightly against her heart.

'It is where you will end up that should be of concern to you,' he said, now standing a metre from her.

His eyes were cut from hazel-coloured marble, she thought. His accent flavoured with a hint of Hindi. Although he spoke quietly, the menace now was definitely worse than before. The last vestigial of hope abandoned her.

'I need you to tell me what you have done with the idol.'

What do I say? she thought. *What is there for me to say?*

'Why did you take it?' he said, crossing the room to lean against the wall with his shoulder, not looking at her but at the curtains, now sealed against the light.

'I didn't, Nora did. I took the bag and ran when your man started to beat us up.'

'Sexton – she said that it was your idea to take the idol, your idea to sell it on – that you said O'Rourke wouldn't have the balls to do anything about it.'

'No,' she whispered, 'it was her idea, not mine. She said those things, I swear to God.'

'It doesn't matter now – where is it?'

'I don't have it,' she said, her breathing laboured. It hurt her to speak. It hurt her to breathe. Hurt her even to think.

'Who… has… it?' he said, each word a driven nail.

She coughed to clear her throat.

'Who?' he said, approaching her.

For such a large man she did not hear the fall of his feet.

He brought his right hand high above his ear. Poised like a shovel. She turned her head away in anticipation of the blow, but his hand did not fall to her face, but elsewhere and he pinched her *there*. Squeezed hard. Pain that she had never felt before surged through her, but before she could scream, he clasped his other hand over her mouth and pressed till she thought her teeth would break anchor from her gums and voyage down her throat. Darkness, then.

CHAPTER 44

So little progress had been made in finding out the whereabouts of Casey. Cohen hadn't been in touch and liaising with the police commander in Jerusalem had proved a useless exercise. No news, and when and *if there is any*, he had said curtly, *we will get in touch with you.*

Resources applied in the search for the missing soldier were thinly spread. The fact that Casey appeared to be missing of her own accord, didn't help improve that particular situation. In their last conversation Cohen said that the Israeli police apparatus was heavily involved in the search: TV news bulletins, newspaper adverts and articles, on-the-ground searches. The UN, on the other hand, had done what exactly? Not much, except pester the Israelis for their not doing enough. The Israeli investigation was not purely altruistic, she understood; they wanted to lay their hands on Casey so as to strip her tongue of what she knew about the smuggling racket, and to discover if she'd access to any more of those freaky idols.

Corrupt and murderous-minded military policemen were involved in searching for Casey, and like the Israelis had their own reasons for finding her. Casey wouldn't come home – she was in dreadful fear for her life, for her UN comrades.

Fredericksen called into the office, looked around.

Emer was writing on the whiteboard, a lead to be followed up.

'Move on it, Captain Harte,' he said. 'Brief me when you have to.'

Then he left.

She'd waited two days for him to say those words.

Moving to her desk, she sat on the swivel chair and said, 'Esther, will you get in touch with Jerusalem MP Detachment and instruct Chief Joseph and Benny to report to the SIS office today? Jo, Albir – Captain Myles O'Rourke, bring him here. Sven... Show me that bag of artefacts that you found during the search in Pollog HQ.'

Figurines of various sizes and shapes, antique gold bracelets with snake heads, silver chest plates, located in a locker formerly owned by Lukas Dabrowski, had been hidden under a false floor, along with a hoard of hash and 300 dollars. Janus had travelled with his brother's remains to Poland, oblivious to the fact his time in the Polish army and consequently with the UN, was over. He wouldn't be returning. A move orchestrated by Fredericksen. She was beginning to believe she wasn't in this mess on her own. Dabrowski's removal happened in the middle of the night, without fanfare, no bugled send-off, no platitudes, no UN-flag-draped coffin. It said nothing much good about him.

Casey... Come home, the hell!

CHAPTER 45

Jenny came to, surfaced slowly to bleak reality; tasted and felt once again the rag in her mouth. Lips sealed with masking tape. It was dark, and she sensed more so than knew for certain that she had been moved to a new location. Thirst, so thirsty.

'Ah, you are with us,' a voice said.

Salah? The Fijian? She could not tell. Then she caught the smell of red onion. Salah. A switch flicked and she saw him. A different room, an office. Shuttered wooden blinds, steel desks, filing cabinets, a naked woman on a wall calendar. June. She heard the faint noise of a forklift and gathered that she was in a warehouse. She had worked in one for a few weeks one summer and this place had that cave-like feel to it. 'I am asking you one more time, yes,' he said, squatting in front of her, peeling back the tape so it hung like a flap of flesh. Extracted the oily rag. His fingernails dirty. Her head sagged; it was as though the column of her neck had simply crumpled. He raised it and looked her straight in the eye. 'Here is how it is for you,' he said. 'If you tell me – it will be over very quickly and your body will be left for your family to find and bury you. You know how it is for families of a family member whose body is not found; they cry for years.'

'I—'

'There is no I for you, anymore; there is only your family.'

'Don't... have... family,' she said between breaths.

'That is a lie,' he said, slapping her cheek lightly. 'You have a mother and a brother.'

'I haven't seen my mother for a long time.'

'But I am sure that you would like a quick death, with little suffering, yes?'

'Kill me and you'll never find it, never.'

'Never? Really, you think that?'

'Water,' she said. 'Please.'

'Maybe you can be sex slave – would you like that, maybe? Every day, you take it for old men with big bellies... Maybe. Then when you full of disease, they take the fun in seeing you die slowly, slowly.'

'Water, please, I need water.'

'No water for you, no,' he said gruffly.

Silence.

Suddenly, she no longer cared.

'I gave... I gave it... to the... Irish officer.'

'Her? The MP? The bitch with the scar?'

'Yes.'

He wiped his lips with the back of his hand, rose to his feet, his knee cracking. Got on the phone and called someone, said, 'She says she gave it to an Irish officer, the woman with the broken nose, it must be. Her. That one you said.'

'Okay,' he said, gazing at his phone at rest on his palm, then looking at her. 'I will get you water. Later.'

He fed her the cloth, sealed over the flap of masking tape. Smiled at her and then left. The blast of open air brought the stink of herself to her nostrils, and this grew in her a profound sense of shame. The door shut with a definitive click.

She struggled violently with her hand and leg restraints. There was no give – she tried again and toppled over from the last flurry of her frantic exertions.

CHAPTER 46

*C*asey, Emer thought. *Is she alive? If so, how is she supporting herself?* Surely she realised, for safety's sake, she should return to her unit. Had she heard of the shootout? Dabrowski's death? Emer had tried her Aunt Gretta but she'd refused to talk with her over the phone. Might a personal visit pay a better dividend? A surprise call in person.

'What information do I need to find out from her?' she murmured.

Some tiny detail that might fit with another piece that would grow into something she could make sense of.

Jenny might have said something to her aunt, the hint of her plan. Aunt Gretta, she now suspected, delivered the idol to her hotel and must know she was embroiled in the case. There could be no distancing of herself from it, ever.

The idol? They would hunt Casey down for it – the buyer, it was said, needed all six to mess with whatever sort of weird mumbo-jumbo they were into. Were the other four idols already in their possession? It appeared so. If that were the case, Emer asked herself, did they receive them from UN personnel? Possibly not, but it was a given they'd done business with each other before. What if they had already caught up with Casey and found she'd disposed of the idol?

There wouldn't be a good outcome for her: playing her only ace, her keep-alive card.

And a worrying development for me, too, Emer thought. *They might believe it was in my possession.*

She was sitting under the mess's bamboo veranda, smoking a cigarillo, drinking a white coffee, a Kit Kat on a paper plate. She stubbed her cigarillo in the ashtray and helped herself to the bar, eating it without enjoying its taste – eating for eating's sake, for distraction.

Stress eating.

This next while would be interesting.

Her frustration radiated from her: at Lahr, toward Sexton and Casey, toward the Dabrowskis, Boland and O'Rourke, the tour leader, the man she had yet to interview because Morris said he was dealing with him for the present. She needed to address that, and today. But not before she'd spoken with someone else.

*

Two hours later, the Fijian did not stand when she entered the interview room. An immediate slight. She let it pass without comment and joined her colleague Sven at the desk; the Norwegian MP whose forehead carried scars of old battles from the boxing ring, whose fight career had followed a similar pattern to Emer's. Injuries had curtailed real promise.

She was surprised at the Fijian's slouched posture, his arms folded. This man was the smile of the place up to a few weeks ago. Now he'd a woeful broodiness about him.

'Master Sergeant Valuba, Joseph,' Emer began, 'this is Sergeant Sven Muller, and we need to put some questions to you.'

'About?' he said, sullenly.

'To begin with; on the date Lieutenant Lahr was shot and wounded, why did you and Staff Sergeant Benny Rafal cross the border at Metula and not via the most logical and practical one of Roshaniqra?'

He shrugged his broad shoulders. 'Because I wanted to attend Mass at Fijibatt HQ in Qana – it was in memory of the massacred.'

In 1996 the Israelis had shelled the UN camp, killing 100 civilians sheltering from the fighting. If so, it made sense for him to use Metula to access Qana.

Sort of turned her line of questioning on its head, as his explanation was entirely plausible. Convincing. Perhaps irrefutable… if she hadn't got her ace.

'In relation to the day of the fatal shooting on the coastal road,' she said, 'were you there?'

'What?'

'Did you drive along the coastal road that day?'

'You can check with the people in Qana,' he said. 'We were at the service.'

'How is the search going for Private Casey?' she said.

'We've been too busy with investigating traffic accidents to do much searching for her.'

'But you did search Akko – yes? And you canvassed as instructed?'

She detected his discomfiture. A wince, a dip of his left eyebrow. Other things she had said had not caused any such reaction.

'Some,' he said. 'We will patrol there again.'

'Did you liaise with the local police in Akko?'

No answer.

'You're aware of the smuggling of antiquities across the border into Israel – has any information about such activity come to your attention?'

'If it had, I would have reported it.'

'And if I were to tell you that your patrol vehicle and you and Benny, were photographed on the coastal road on the day of the fatal shooting, what would you say?'

Sven placed a photograph under Chief Joseph's nose, identical to the one that Esther and Jo were currently showing to Benny in another room.

'Take a few moments to think on that,' she said.

He could shrug it off, say 'so what?' What did it mean? Nothing. They were swanning around, on a drive. Big deal. But she knew he wouldn't admit to any such thing, because his mind was busy trying to suss if she had more on him than the photograph. Photographs that came to her as a courtesy thank-you from Avi Cohen. The Israelis still had a foot presence in Lebanon. At this very moment Traffic Section were recovering the Jeep driven from the scene, from the UN scrapyard on an offroad a kilometre before the border crossing.

'Well,' she pressed.

He remained silent.

'Right at this moment,' she said, 'the Israeli police are arresting some of their custom officials and soldiers at both crossing points.' She paused and continued, 'And we are busy arresting several of our own MPs.'

His eyes drilled into hers. She did not flinch.

He said calmly, 'Am I under arrest?'

'Yes,' she said, 'most definitely. As of now.' She advised him of his right to remain silent, and said, 'Have you anything to say?'

'No comment?'

'Where is the idol?'

'No comment.'

'Do you know where Private Casey is?'

'No comment.'

She glanced at Sven, a signal for him to accompany Chief Joseph to the cells, to go through the necessary procedures for his detention. Benny would also be arrested, but he would be detained elsewhere in camp; she didn't want the pair to meet.

A hectic day, with prospects of it becoming more hectic before day's end.

'Oh and Sven, tell Captain Myles O'Rourke that I want to see him... please.'

The tour organiser had been left to stew in the mess, where he could see the comings and goings. She'd so much yearned to grow huge worry in him.

CHAPTER 47

O'Rourke sat with his chair pushed back from the desk. She thought his hands small, insectile fingers long and slender, nails chewed to the quick. Mister Antiquities himself.

'You're in a bit of trouble, Myles,' Emer said, 'but I think you already know that, right?'

'I organised the tours, which was my remit.' Waving her question away, his hand like a leaf caught on a solo breath of wind.

'Don't,' she warned.

'Don't what?'

'Here's the situation – your name has repeatedly come up in statements taken from border military police and from Israeli customs officials. Haven't you seen the flurry of activity in our camp? We have three cells holding four prisoners. A billet is serving as another cell.'

He averted his eyes.

'Within the next hour, those cells will be empty and the men will be under lock and key in their own battalion areas in the hills – so I will have plenty of room for you.'

'Colonel Morris will—'

'He won't save you.'

Just as he was about to speak, the door to the SIS office opened and Sven beckoned to her.

'Esther, would you make Captain O'Rourke a tea or better yet, a strong coffee? It might waken his brain cells.'

Once the door was closed Sven whispered, 'We let him make a call.'

'And?'

Emer had allowed Sven to place a listening device in the form of a double adaptor in the office where Chief Joseph was left to stew. What information they might glean wouldn't be permissible evidence at a court-martial – in fact, it was illegal – but it could give her vital leverage.

She'd mooted the proposal at a staff briefing and Sven mentioned he had a surveillance kit: a travel adaptor housing a small transmitter. No one raised an objection. These people were young but experienced police officers in their respective countries – they knew that information gained through illicit means sometimes saved on a lot of man-hours and endless guesswork. This situation warranted riding the rules a little – a soldier was missing, there'd been a death, and Lahr wasn't out of the woods.

...We need intel.

She hadn't appraised Fredricksen in case he vetoed the plan.

Sven thumbed the Pressel on his Dictaphone, index finger raised like it were a detonator.

'Listen... Listen... Salah... Say nothing to me... except yes,' 'then you go, clear off.'

'That's it,' Sven said. 'I have the number he called, but...' He shrugged as if to say whoever the big Fijian called had gone to ground. They would buy a new phone or a SIM card.

She said, feeble-spirited, 'We still have no idea if Casey is still alive.'

Emer returned to the office. Coolly, she watched O'Rourke sip at his coffee. Outside, on the base's main road, a convoy of trucks passed the MP camp, slowing over a speed ramp, the *thump-thump* of the wheels punctuating the silence. She wondered if he would break cover and reveal what he knew, or would he clam up and wait it out to see what it was that they had on him? The convoy rumbled on and the road fell quiet, the atmosphere further defiled by the slow, whiny breath of the fan on top of a filing cabinet.

'Well?' Emer pushed.

He coughed, shook his head as though to suggest he was not sure which way to turn.

'We have you in the picture,' she said. 'You can either cooperate or choose not to.'

'Shouldn't you caution me if you think I've committed a crime? I read that somewhere, I think,' he said sarcastically. 'Where was it? Ah – The Defence Act, 1954.'

'I haven't decided that you have done anything wrong. People allege that you are corrupt and have said so in their statements, but they could be fabrications... That's why I'd like your side of the matter. Before I make a judgement call.'

He sighed.

'Are they?' she asked.

'Show me the statements – who said I was corrupt? How dare they?'

'You can't see the statements – not yet. Later, your defence team can show them to you. They're singing, Myles, trust me. Like a drunken batch of New Year's Eve revellers.'

He remained silent.

'I'm entitled to arrest you if I suspect that you've committed a crime. That's in the Defence Act, too. If I do that, I'll be citing your failure to help me with my inquiries into locating a missing Irish soldier.'

'I don't know where she is. If I did...'

'I want to know everything you did and everyone that you met during the course of your smuggling activities. I'd start right now, if I were you. It's in your best interest, really.'

He stared at her with eyes that had begun to well and started to talk.

CHAPTER 48

Emer thought it had come as a huge relief for him to unburden himself. He'd spoken self-pityingly of his financial problems, his gambling addiction, his debts to moneylenders, which in turn led him to rely on Quartermaster Hughie Boland, who charged him exorbitant interest rates for the privilege. An officer doesn't borrow money from the junior ranks. If word leaked, O'Rourke's career would have sailed down the Liffey into the Irish Sea. And his banker Boland knew this. That is how it started. In Lebanon, Boland showed him a means of writing off his debt. They started with shipping small antiquities over the border to test the system – Boland and the Dabrowski brothers; ensured the right people were in situ to dramatically lessen the risks. Everyone going across carried one or two pieces. Everyone? The revelation astounded Emer. It meant that a minimum of 15 to a maximum of 23 had smuggled artefacts into Israel on five tours sanctioned by the UN. Some of the personnel, like Sexton and Casey, were repeat travellers, but many others were not. It was going to prove a logistical nightmare to locate the personnel involved, many of whom were perhaps now in their home countries, believing themselves safe from prosecution. And they were, most likely; proving they'd engaged in criminal wrongdoing could be next to impossible.

So many tributaries, she thought as she knocked on Fredericksen's door to brief him. She half expected her commanding officer to reprimand her for the bugging set-up; he was bound to hear of it sometime.

'Come in,' he said, addressing her rapping.

He was on the phone to Morris when she entered. 'Yes, Gerry.'

He was addressing the Irish officer by his first name. She sat in the chair as he wrapped up the call.

'So?' he said quietly.

He did not lose it, which she considered a curious turn, when briefed of the adaptor ruse; just nodded several times very slowly as though carefully balancing the news. Emer remembered he had once conceded that police sometimes had to do murky things if they wanted results. She'd fussed over nothing.

'So, he wants a deal, our chief,' he said.

There was a wariness to him that she had not seen before. A strain to his features, a moistness in his usually frosty eyes.

She said, 'Yes, I suppose he does, if he can cut one.'

'He realises that a deal might not be possible if Timo doesn't make it.'

'I would think it forms part of his thinking, yes. If he tells us of Casey's whereabouts and she's alive. Well, these would be primary conditions for a deal.'

She found the notion of a deal repugnant, in spite of its major benefit.

Fredericksen reflected. 'He's being transferred to his battalion in Fijibatt and his superiors will court-martial him... I suspect, given his status, he'll be treated lightly.'

'He's involved in a kidnapping and is an accessory to attempted murder, perhaps one murder if Timo...'

'Have we proof? At best he is facing charges for being in receipt of stolen goods. Is there proof that isn't circumstantial? Sergeant Benny... Has Rafal said anything?'

'He's incriminated himself and Chief Joseph in relation to being absent without leave from MP Jerusalem Detachment. And we have statements from others linking him, Boland, O'Rourke and the Dabrowskis as the ringleaders of the smuggling operation.'

Fredericksen said nothing. Harte could not really judge but it was as though he wanted advice on how to smother the investigation.

'Sir, we have possibly over 40 UN soldiers who smuggled high-end and valuable antiquities into Israel, most of which were stolen and looted from Iraqi museums.'

'I am only too well aware. I hear this every day at least five times from high-ranking officers. It's going to make the UN, and us, look very bad.'

Pressure from on high to take the heat off somehow, someway, she thought. *Morris is one of those on-high men.*

He said, 'Can we presume that our former MPs have the idols?'

'Blank faces when we asked. But I assume they have one, or they at least did…'

'Which leaves one unaccounted for. The one Casey stole.'

'Fled for her life with it, I would think. It wasn't on her mind to desert.'

'Seemingly,' he agreed, meeting her gaze. He went on, 'Your senior Irish officer, Gerry, he is very impressed with the level of cooperation given to us by this Detective Avi Cohen.'

'It's mutual police cooperation, sir,' she said.

'In what way is it mutual?'

'A professional way, of course, extending professional courtesy – he asked Lahr and I if we were going to do something about the border smuggling and when I said no, Cohen said, "Good." So what the Israelis have now done, they'd been intending to do for some time.'

He poured a glass of water from a jug and held the cup thoughtfully.

She said, 'Shouldn't we be discussing Casey and how we should get her back – and not a flipping figurine?'

He drank the water slowly to the last drop and squashed the cup.

He said, 'Casey is dead.'

Her lips opened but she was stunned speechless.

'Her body was found washed up against the rocks in Akko about an hour ago,' he said.

CHAPTER 49

As it turned out, the people got it wrong, she told Hannah on the phone later. The body was not that of Casey but of a woman roughly her age, wearing an Irish army T-shirt with Casey's cloth nametag and private rank markings. The unfortunate was a young Columbian woman by the name of Selena, who had stayed at the Century Youth Hostel. Emer guessed that Jenny had been lying low there – it should have been better checked out by the MPs and Israeli police. Avi insisted it had been visited, adding that the Irish woman was more resourceful than many in such dire circumstances.

Chief Joseph refused to answer questions she'd put to him; even the prospect of a deal no longer appealed – he would take his chances with his own. He was, after all, a chief with clout back in Fiji. At present he was detained in Qana, Fijibatt Headquarters, lying low, awaiting repatriation, she suspected. Rafal was already in Poland.

CHAPTER 50

Blurry-eyed, aching all over, Jenny squinted against a burst of daylight. Her left eye pinched from the closing. Cable tied to the chair, lying on its side, hands behind her back.

Words Aunt Gretta said zipped to mind: *Old bones tell no lies; they're the devil in disguise.* If she survived this load of dung, her bones would be prematurely old.

Exhausted, perspiring, lips dry and cut. A bell sounded in her head, louder than the one in Notre Dame – an image of the movie flashed across her mind. Anthony Hopkins played the hunchback and she cried while watching it, feeling his pain, his utter despair at loving a woman who could not love him in return, at least not with the sort of love he had in his heart for her.

She felt herself sliding into sleep or unconsciousness – she was not sure which, only that she must not allow it to happen.

Her mouth contained a filthy piece of cloth. She recalled Salah feeding it to her, but then he was distracted when his phone sounded. She sensed it was something serious as a creeping panic seized his features. Salah put his fingertips to his temple as though to arrest some negative thought or a flash of pain. He was no longer in control. He left in a hurry but still thought to turn the key behind him.

A mouse. She watched it scurrying along the grey skirting board and disappear behind a filing cabinet. She tried to move but the slide along the blue linoleum was fractional. If she could manage to expel the rag... *Only get rid of these bastarding cable ties.* Only do all of that before Salah returned.

Must try. Must.

She rocked herself back and forth, clawing at the floor with her fingers, trying to propel herself forward... Stop, go... Stop and go. Making progress ever so slowly, hurting ever so much, trying to push away thoughts of despair, of asking herself what next?

What does she do after reaching the wall?

There now, mucus running from her nostrils, perspiration stinging her eyes, she pressed her forehead against the coffee-stained blue plaster. Again she rocked back and forth, this time bringing her head from the wall and angling the chair's legs for a push forward. Once, twice, another, she slid the chair hard against the wall. Suddenly there was a wrench, a noisy splintering. The back leg of the chair... but not broken, not yet.

Dredging strength from deep within, she forced the chair harder and heard the final give. Her left leg was free. She stretched her knee a little, bringing on pins and needles, and she had to endure those... crying and laughing at the same time, detesting the sensation. Unable to proceed further until it had passed, next, she set to breaking the other legs, succeeding and finally managing to stand, hunched.

She was poor deaf Quasimodo with a fiddleback chair for a hump. She stared at the detritus on the floor she had kicked against. Plaster pieces and dust. This time she swung her 'hump' against the blue wall and felt – on the third attack – the chair sundering. Stopped. Her eyes bulged from the effort. The traffic of air in and out of her nostrils maddened her further; her harsh breathing worsened the pain in her ribcage and her throat. Every part of her sounded as a chorus of pain.

She stood, leaned her back against the wall. Her hands, bound behind her, prevented her from doing what she most wanted: to drag that cloth from her mouth. The cables about her ankles were loose, since parting from the chair legs.

Instinctively, in temper, she stepped back from the wall, and kicked at it, kicked and kicked until she'd created a hole the size of a manhole cover. Staring through the gap, she saw desks, chairs, boxes of photocopying paper, reams of different coloured paper, brochures, standing fans – a mesh window cut cubes of sunlight onto the floor and the opposite wall. Wriggling through, she straightened herself and hurried to the drawer of the largest desk, but saw what she needed before opening it. On the dusty walnut surface, in a red holder for pens and suchlike, a black-handled pair of scissors. Using her foot she drew the knick-knack holder to her, turned her back and...

Five bites of the scissors cut through the cable. She paused, staring at the rag in her hand, gagging for water, to wash away the taste – erase the image of Salah's thick fingers inserted in her mouth.

She retched but nothing came, not even when she thought of the big man and what he had done to her. Now that she was free, she was unable to move. A mess.

How can I walk down the streets like this?

She cut the ties around her ankles – a sharp pain stabbed her lower back.

A navy jacket hung from a peg on a coat stand in a corner, also a football jersey, a khaki satchel bag, a sun umbrella. Underneath these were red *Gola* trainers and work boots, dry and stiff from an age of unuse.

She rammed the jersey into the empty bag, the light rain jacket. *What else?*

Nothing.

Get out.

Listen.

Noise. The fall of feet. But not rushing; slow – in no hurry to be anywhere.

The window.

She pushed a chair flush to the wall, levered the handle and lifted the latch. Extended the window with one hand, pushing against the mesh wire with the other. It yielded easily.

Hoisting herself up, she pushed the bag ahead of her and

wriggled through. She fell a short distance onto concrete, amid an apron of oil barrels.

I can't take much more. I really fucking can't.

It was late; the sun was setting. It would be dark within a few heartbeats.

Where to?

She limped through the sprawling and empty industrial estate. Heard a train pass by, quite close. *The state of me. I'll draw attention to myself... Find someplace to rest, to clean up, someplace.*

Here was nowhere. Something you'd see in a horror movie, with zombies popping awake left, right, and centre.

She headed in the direction of the train's clickety-clacking, sensing she would find an embankment there, where she could rest, sleep.

Forget.

CHAPTER 51

In the pre-dawn, a howling dog awakened Jenny Casey. She lay on her back, eyes focused on the stars, wishing she had a cigarette and a hot whiskey to hand. A spliff, even. Or a pill that would help her mind to dance, make her feel good. Numb the different pains. She sat up, suddenly anxious about snakes and spiders, things she had been too tired to worry about when she'd reached this place. She had lain down and conked out.

She was clueless about what she should do next. She had no money. She was hungry and thirsty, sore and bleeding from her gums and vagina; a tooth was gone, her lips swollen, eyes ached. In the letter she had left for Aunt Gretta, she'd begged her to consider something – and she, in turn, would be forever grateful. Casey could not return to service life, simply couldn't face a court-martial, being drummed out of the army, answering questions until she was blue in the face – and those men – they were dangerous and would hunt for her till the end of time. If she could, please help? Help her big-time. *I'm not like my mother. I swear it, Gretta.*

But she had no money to call and find out if Gretta was of a heart to help. Neither had she a clue where she was, nor much energy to spend on searching for directions to the kibbutz at Qiryat Shmona.

Zipping up her jacket, she set off. On the brow of the embankment, she looked down at the back gardens of a row of houses. Behind her, a train chugged, lazily strumming the rails. She limped her way past the houses, wandered right at the last one and kept going. She turned when she heard a tractor lumbering behind her, pulling a flatbed trailer. Stuck her thumb out and watched the driver pass by; a heavyset woman, who in an afterthought, braked about 10 metres away. Jenny had already given up and resumed limping.

The woman struggled to contain her alarm upon seeing the hiker up close.

'You should go to a hospital. I can make a call for you, if you would like?' the woman said.

Jenny waved no, caught a whiff of herself that made her gag in disgust. *I'm reeking.*

'Okay. I can drop you close to Tiberias. Once you're on the road to it, you can take a bus. They come by regularly on that road. But... you need to see a doctor.'

She spoke in a mid-western American accent, with a light blue scarf on her short brown hair, and her fair skin was sun lotioned, scented with a mild fragrance of rosewater.

Jenny indicated she could not speak.

'You're dumb?'

You better believe it, she thought, as she nodded. Dumb in more ways than one.

Tiberias. Good. Closer to Gretta.

The woman side glanced her passenger several times. Jenny noticed but kept her gaze fixed on the road ahead, then her eyes went to the trailer and its cargo of empty wooden crates. On the slats were images of oranges. Jenny tasted the juice...

'Here,' the woman said, pushing a 10-shekel note at her at the turn-off point. Their eyes met. 'It's not much – but you make sure to do the same for someone else, pass it on, right?'

'Right,' said Jenny before she could stop herself.

The woman smiled and said, 'It's a miracle.'

Jenny thought so, too.

'You can speak.'

No, the real miracle was this woman's decision to stop, and that Jenny now had a little money to move forward. She was about to make for the road when the sprinklers in the fields came on, and instead, she went there to drink and clean herself as best she could. In the back of her mind was the belief the woman would call the cops. An afterthought, like her picking up a hitchhiker.

CHAPTER 52

Three weeks later and Emer'd just signed off on the interim report resting on her desk. The case would make a large and significant tome when finally submitted. First up was a 25-plus-page Final Investigation Report, twice as many statements, as well as injury reports, maps, photograph albums, and video evidence. There were problems with a few of the statements recorded by her staff, with grammar and punctuation not adequately expressing what a witness had said. Some had to be retaken, some written by the witness's own hand and in their own tongue – and when translated made less sense. The end product was most likely to read, perhaps not in relation to Casey (it's not a crime to go missing, is it?), '...*to date no one has been found amenable for this crime. Should further information come to light, a report will be submitted.'*

It rankled with Emer how close the phrase read to what Lahr had suggested she write.

Fredericksen was investigating the ambush and he had things much easier; he had culprits – one dead, one alive. He could wrap up his report with a positive conclusion, a genuine final report. His difficulty lay in how to write up his report without tainting Lahr's reputation and by association the UN's. Typical, she thought for most organisations; keep the light shining through the shit.

The smuggling racket was now old hat. Fredericksen was on leave, back in Norway. Morris hadn't spoken very much to her since the false scare about Casey's death, and she figured he had other worries on his mind.

She had rented a small apartment in Nahariya, about fifteen

minutes' drive from the border. She did not want to spend a year living in a military environment, not 24/7. Caged in like a zoo animal.

Emer believed she'd put the Investigation Section on an even keel and on top of things. Now and then she welled up a little at the thoughts of Lahr – like Fredericksen with his report, she intended lying. She would refrain from mentioning the 'bribe' money she'd found in his desk, and she would not share her suspicion that Lahr appeared to be aware of many aspects of what would unfold on that grim day. Whereas the Dabrowskis and others were motivated by greed, Lahr erred because he needed money to pay for his daughter's medical bills. She considered donating the bribe money to an orphanage. 15,000 USD would be a massive help for one she had in mind in the hills of Lebanon. Gifted anonymously, or perhaps buy a minibus outright and just park it with keys outside the home? Leave a card.

Best idea may be the latter, as cash vanishes. In any regard, she would not use a cent of it for personal use.

She glanced up at the clock; not long till visiting hours at the hospital. She'd visit Timo, then come back to do a little work before crossing the border.

CHAPTER 53

Lahr was in no doubt that Fredericksen and Emer had done too much for him, and he was grateful for it. As soon as he was able, he would be home with his little Jacki. He couldn't wait. She was what kept him going. When he said this, Emer felt a little like she was being put in her place, not intentionally – he just hadn't got her in his sights when it came to romance. It made her feel foolish because she had thought there might have been a flicker of interest.

He was still weak from the loss of blood. The wound had developed an infection and then another, but now looked to be healing. He'd lost weight and his arms and legs were slightly atrophied.

Some days after regaining consciousness he revealed the missing segments; Lukas Dabrowski wanted her dead – but it wasn't supposed to happen like that – the idol would be handed over, he would give her 15,000 as part of her cut, persuade her to accept it. That way neither she nor her sister Hannah would be harmed – that was the agreement. Whatever about herself, they reckoned she would not endanger her sister. But Janus Dabrowski had ordered otherwise. She'd stirred a hornets' nest within that man. Prideful and misogynistic, murderous.

She asked, 'What about your cut?'

'I posted it to my mother from the French Base Post Office, stuffed inside a teddy for Jacki – she loves teddies – Baloo the Bear – she loves him...'

'How much?'

'Fifteen thousand, also.'

'Christ... I don't know where this puts us.'

She felt stupid for saying it – there was no 'us'. How could there be?

His face held a momentary surprise, like he'd caught sight of a butterfly in winter.

She said the grapes were a little too sweet. His lips looked parched and she poured him some water.

'I'll be out of here in a week or so,' he said. 'I was lucky… As soon I get some strength back, I'll go home.'

She nodded.

'I want to thank you again, Emer, for all you've done. My mother said she met you several times when you visited me here… When I was in a coma.'

A quiet woman, tall, kind face, with long blonde hair she was allowing to turn grey.

Kristen had told her in confidence, 'Jacki isn't going to make it. When it happens, will you tell him? It would be better if he heard from someone he knows, than hearing the news over the phone, or from a stranger.'

'Oh, my god,' Emma had said.

'Is it too much to ask?'

It was. It is.

'Maybe you will visit,' he said. 'I would love for you to come to see us. I was talking to Jacki last night – she sounded very weak, wants me home, crying – breaks my heart to hear her breaking down, you know… What about it?'

'Do you Skype?' she voiced, worried; if he saw Jacki he would be inconsolable.

'No, my mother isn't into technology – she can just about manage to text. I've asked her to get in a neighbour or one of my brothers to show her. But everyone is so busy with their own lives.'

Ah, they defer, put him off, she thought.

He squeezed her hand in gratitude.

Had he meant the invitation, was something he felt he should say? she thought.

'I will pay for your ticket,' he said.

She snapped, jokingly, 'You will in your arse. I'll pay for my own.'

Her smile lit his.

CHAPTER 54

Emer struggled to suppress a yawn. She checked her watch, picked up her satchel, loaded it with the file, her laptop, and left the office. She did not lock up as some staff were due back from a random search on homeward-bound troops at the airport. Polish troops, as it turned out.

It was late. 0945. The border would close in fifteen minutes.

Speed up, there. Get home, soak in the bath, unwind.

After crossing into Israel, she shifted gears out of a bad curve and drove quickly. Her head beams dipped in marked contrast to the car behind her, illuminating her car interior.

'He's too bloody close for comfort,' she murmured.

Flashed her hazards, but the following car still poured full head beams. Farther on, she indicated to pull over, but the vehicle slowed, keeping behind her. Increasing speed, she weighed her options.

Police station?

No.

Radio?

Who?

They intended frightening her; to let her know they hadn't forgotten about her. Another night, another time, no head beams would alert her to their presence.

Her turn-off junction for home lay ahead, and she veered right without indicating.

This way was a minor road; railway tracks bisected it close to her apartment block.

So much for thinking of a glass of wine and a smoke on the balcony as she looked out at the sea.

She braked gently in front of the dropped boom, watched a train trundling past, carriages swaying slightly. After the last one passed she checked her side-view mirror.

Same car?

Deffo. Silver. Honda, maybe.

She drove past the apartment, took the next left and then a right, meeting traffic lights on red. Indicated left and drove past the Carlton Hotel and the Penguin Bar on Hage'aton Boulevard. Still in her side mirror, the Honda. At the top of the street, she thought to use the Motorola to contact MP Coy, but decided against, going with her gut instinct.

Merely doing this to scare me?

It hit her like a slap from the dark.

They believe you still have the idol.

This was the reason she hadn't been taken out. Revenge for killing Luka Dabrowski would have to wait.

Is he here? Janus? No... No... He's in Poland. Isn't he?

Turning her saloon right onto the Akko road, she did a double take in her mirror.

Akko, where they thought Casey's body had been found snagged in rocks on the beach.

Nine clicks to the old city, where Saladin broke the Crusaders' hold on the Levant. And yes, the car was still tailing her. A driver used to the task.

She indicated left and watched in her mirror the chasing car do likewise. But she kept going straight, increasing speed, climbing gears to the roundabout, and circling it, heading back toward Nahariya, keeping a check on the oncoming traffic to see if the silver car had followed.

But she'd made enough ground and had lost them this time.

After locking the patio door Emer settled into an armchair on the balcony, a thin, tawny-coloured blanket wrapped over her knees. In the morning, she would ring Avi to make him aware of what had happened. Maybe he could find out who the tail was, and how best to proceed. She could report the incident to Fredericksen when he got back, but he might order her across the border to live. She did not want that and anyhow, Hannah was due to visit soon. Hannah would come out, no matter what; she so loved the fucking *Holy Land*.

She smoked and drank wine. The merlot did little to unravel the knot in her stomach. She did not have a sidearm as UN personnel weren't permitted to carry firearms in Israel. Even if she were, her service pistol had been removed from the armoury and packaged as evidence for Boland's court-martial.

Neither Morris nor Fredericksen had told her this and she felt a pinch of guilt, as though she were open to question about the shootout. It was correct protocol she knew, but she'd no reason to feel guilty. She'd been defending herself and her partner, but still there was guilt bordering on shame. Shame at the blood on her hands. Even if it belonged to mercenary lowlifes.

She had, hadn't she, shot Dabrowski as he lay on the ground, having shot the legs from under him? This would be put to her at the inquest. Why? Response? She'd believed he was still a threat to her life. Shield the fact that something cold inside her had taken over, something chilling, a side to herself she scarcely knew, because she had never before been in such an extremely hostile situation. She could have frozen; she didn't. If she had, she'd most likely be dead.

Emer stared at the half-moon until her neck began to ache; lowered her eyes to a ship's lights on the horizon, bound for Haifa. She remembered a visit to Mount Carmel overlooking the port, and the stench from the city's salt mines, like sulphur wafting into her nostrils.

Speculated. What became of the idol Lahr had in his bag on that fateful trip? Quizzing Chief Joseph on the matter, he had asked her what the hell she was talking about. Benny shook his head, then shrugged and said he had no idea. Neither claimed to have seen it, which could be true. They had no reason to lie, not now. Equally they had no reason to assist her with her enquiries. Neither was Hughie Boland going to furnish her with information, not to the woman who had taken away a limb. Myles O'Rourke had confirmed the existence of two idols and that he'd carried both across the border. He was paid three grand for each. He'd no idea who supplied the merchandise; that was down to the Dabrowskis and Boland. She didn't believe him. He was an expert in antiquities and probably a lean-to man for the Polish brothers. A bit of a cute hoor, O'Rourke – her father would often say that of a man whom he secretly half admired.

The call to Cohen was brief. He issued her with the same advice that Fredericksen would have done. Either stay in the UN camp or have someone come live with her, even if only to act as another pair of eyes. Dissuading Hannah from coming had proved futile; Hannah refused to listen to, 'No.' Or, 'another time, yeah?' Or, 'Leave it, for now, okay?'

Exasperated, Emer said, 'Hannah, for God's sake, your life is under threat.'

'What?'

'Yes. You moron – listen up.'

'I don't care, I'm so excited. I have the holiday booked and the ticket paid for.'

'Hannah.'

'I'm packed. I'll care about that other stuff when I'm there.'

There's no getting through to her.

She isn't listening. I can't get her to.

A Polish psychopath is off the leash and baying for my blood and that of anyone connected to me.

On the other hand: there are no borders, no haven... She could be caught at home as easily as here...

'Okay, okay.' Emer sighed her surrender.

CHAPTER 55

Emer varied her routine over the following week and hadn't noticed anything suspicious. Often, she'd think about where to go next with the Jenny Casey investigation and then abruptly switch to her own personal safety.

Not a clue which way to turn with the investigation. There were no reported sightings of the missing soldier. It was as though she'd vanished from the face of the earth.

Emer often found herself looking at young women who matched Casey's age and build, wondering if that were her. Quizzing, hoping, wishing they were, that chance and not investigation would solve the missing person case. Understood too that Casey could stand six feet from her in a group and she'd be unable to distinguish her from the others. Photographs lie and she would have changed her appearance. Dramatically, for sure. If she were still on the run, that is, and not...

The calendar indicated the new month. August 1.

She was collecting Hannah at Ben Gurion Airport and dropping her straight to the apartment. She could rest until she got back from meeting Fredericksen. He had called her to his office for a private meeting.

What now?

To lay accountability; was it her fault Lahr was badly injured? That she had killed Lukas Dabrowski? That they hadn't managed to locate Jenny Casey? Morris had gone to ground entirely. At times she felt isolated, tarnished, pushed to the margin. What if she were cracking up and needed help? Who could she turn to? Her sister? Too weak. Lahr? No. Not yet, at any rate. Lone rider... Ghosted by her peers. Not by the people she'd put behind bars.

CHAPTER 56

Hannah, she thought, had considerably aged since she'd last seen her in McKee Barracks, on the morning she was setting off for Lebanon. Her hair, cut short and dyed a light brown was in marked contrast to what it had been in Dublin – but then Hannah always liked to try different hairstyles. Her eyes lacked their familiar sparkle and her smile seemed forced.

A bad flight?

Jet lag?

Strain there. Absolutely.

They chatted as Emer breezed them along the route, falling silent for a patch until Hannah breathed the words Jerusalem and Nazareth as they passed road signs. Reverently, in a tone that piqued her older sister. For her, those places did not hold the same currency.

Emer got the impression Hannah regretted getting here 2,000 years late and missing the big event. Hannah had always clutched at rosary beads in times good or bad. She had given Emer a set made from green Connemara marble to keep her safe in Lebanon. No doubt, she'd lit countless candles for her sister. Such concern took the edge off Emer's rising irritation. But how Hannah had kept the faith after the Curragh discovery of G.I.'s mother, she could never grasp. For her, that day, God left by the back door and never returned.

The sun was glorious. Fields full of cotton. Zipping right to head north, away from Tel Aviv, Emer decided to slide in a question.

'So, how are things with you?'

'Fine.'

'No, I mean really?'

'Really fine,' Hannah responded, glancing at her sister.

That look, Emer thought. *Things are not good.*

Don't push her. Not yet.

'Hannah... I've got to go into work – I'll be gone for about a couple of hours – to meet with the boss. You don't mind...? I've got plenty of food in, and wine... Beer...'

'Okay...'

'It's just that... he wants a briefing...'

'I'll be grand – don't be worrying.'

This could be a long few weeks, or very short. Then it came to mind that her sister's luggage was more in keeping with someone going on a fortnight's holiday, not for months as she'd asserted. Emer hadn't said anything – that was for a face-to-face talk.

*

Colonel Fredericksen toyed with the wedding band on his left hand as he listened to her briefing, the last to be given by the company's section heads. He'd listened intently to reports from the Provost Platoon, Traffic Section, Transport Unit, Detachment Commanders – AKA the Dogfaces – from Beirut, Tyre, Nahariya and Jerusalem (in absentia). By the end of her briefing, he was nodding slowly, like a drawn-out sentence leading to a full stop. When he stopped nodding, he asked Emer to stay behind. He thanked everyone else for their contribution, prior to laying down a few of what he called steadfast rules; reminders, he said – he would not tolerate the law enforcers being lawbreakers. No one would be treated lightly if they disregarded the rules and his orders were that – orders, not requests. No mixed signals.

She watched the others exit the operations room. There was a moving of chairs to ease departure, some comments voiced underneath in national tongues – French, Italian, Finnish and Norwegian.

He came from behind his desk and sat on its edge.

'I have something for you, but tell me what, if anything, you could not say in front of the others.'

She offloaded once again her frustration at the dead-end she found herself in with the Casey disappearance. She held back from mentioning Avi Cohen – no choice, really, as he spoke over her to say, 'And the death of Dabrowski.'

Is this a statement or a question of sorts? she thought.

He said, 'It was necessary for you to shoot him?'

Statement or question?

His eyes did not leave her and she said, not short of sarcasm, 'I only shoot people whenever it is absolutely necessary.'

He moved his head to the side as though he'd just received a mild slap. Straightened up and returned to his seat. 'Good, I think it was always going to be necessary for someone to shoot him sometime. I had to ask – you will be asked in a more hostile setting in a more hostile manner. I want to ask one more thing.'

'Sir?

'Why did you shoot him a second time, after you'd brought him down?'

'I was angry, terrified, and I didn't know if I'd incapacitated his ability to try and kill me.'

He adjusted his brown tie, another twist on the ring finger. 'Good. Good. You do not need me to tell you that you are at risk – I have done much research on those men and Janus will want to avenge his brother's death. If he does not, he will lose face in front of those who do the majority of his dirty work. He has to be the King Dirty. You understand?'

'He's in Poland,' she said, nerves coming to her voice, 'or so I was told.'

'Poland is not the other side of the moon.'

'I know, but—'

'And he still has compatriots here on this base.' He paused and added, 'What is keeping you alive is that you have something that he sees as his property.'

'I don't.'

'It doesn't matter whether you do or not, Janus believes it. He would take it from you and then dispose of you as he had done with others. There's a trace of blood from Iraq to here.'

'How should I handle things?'

'Excuse my language, Emer, but when we deal with a piece of shit, we need to know the tricks of the sewer. Think outside of the box, always. Be careful, have no routine, and perhaps you should carry a weapon. If this is possible. This is what I have to ask you; if I get permission for you, will you carry a weapon? Something small. You are still residing off base?'

'Yes, I have my sister staying with me,' she said, 'and I would carry a pistol, of course.'

'Your sister is staying... with you?'

'Yes.'

'Do you think that's a good idea?'

'I warned her – I couldn't stop her. She could be got at in Ireland, too. Isn't that so?'

'Hmm... We'll talk again. Keep me posted and if you need to talk before I get back to you, yes, you'll do that, call me? ...I was also going to suggest you reside in base until... But your sister... Be careful.'

CHAPTER 57

Travelling to Nahariya, her thoughts dwelled on the idol's long, dark shadow. It and its cousin had wreaked havoc with people's lives – she began to believe the objects might indeed be cursed. Dabrowski paid the highest price, perhaps Casey too. Boland lost his limb; others would lose rank and reputation. She had lost what?

Something. She wasn't sure what it was, yet. *Still at stake is my life, maybe Hannah's. Isn't that enough to be getting on with?*

Chasing echoes. Chasing something that couldn't be seen, only heard. Sometimes she found herself thinking and imagining that Casey was alive, and then the crime scene photos of the innocent woman's washed-up remains would flash like lightning. A huge sense of deflation would drip feed into her veins and leave her with the abject feeling of having let Casey down. She must be dead.

Yet, what more could she have done? What could she have done better from the outset? Fear kept Casey from handing herself in, a fear that had blown her into an alleyway with a dead end. A pity. What a pity.

Three people were aware of Emer's involvement with that hideous-looking artefact: Casey, her Aunt Gretta who hand delivered it at the hotel's reception desk, and Avi Cohen. Avi wouldn't talk and she doubted whether Aunt Gretta would implicate herself by saying she'd delivered the piece to Emer's hotel. What about the receptionist? Would he have told someone about her receiving a package? Rule these out of the equation and the likely and most plausible answer was that the truth had been painfully extracted from Casey.

I was too slow in taking Chief Joseph and Benny in for interviewing. Should have done that when I saw the Fijian's threatening behaviour towards Pedney.

Perhaps I could have learned something from conducting those interviews?

Checked her mirrors. Empty of chasers. Indicated.

A weapon, he had said. Not a good sign.

She took it to mean that an attack on her was imminent. It didn't matter which side of the border she was on; it didn't matter if she was in Ireland. Poland wasn't a far-off planet...

CHAPTER 58

Hannah had changed out of her travel clothes into navy shorts and a blue tank top. She sat out on the balcony in the cool evening breeze that carried a heady scent of salt and seaweed. She looked up at Emer when the patio door slid back.

'Can I get you something?' Emer asked gently, thinking she was upsetting Hannah's peace and tranquillity.

'No, I have the vino.'

'Crisps?'

'Ah, maybe. I brought Tayto. Will I—'

Emer's favourite.

'Sit, Hannah. I'll get them...'

'They're on the bed.'

After grabbing the six-pack of cheese and onion crisps, Emer poured herself a whiskey, picked up a sandwich from the plate she'd left for Hannah, and joined her sister.

'How did the meeting go? What's he like?' Hannah asked.

Her lean freckled face shone with moisturizer. Her forearms, Emer thought much thinner than she remembered.

'He was okay, nicer to me than he was before. It's a little hard to tell what sort he is at any time.'

Hannah gazed over the parapet at the stars above the horizon. Palm fronds in the corner of the balcony shivered in an almost imperceptible breeze.

'How are you?' Emer asked, patting her shirt pocket, frowning.

Her cigarillos were in the car. Thought then that she might have a packet in the apartment. Where?

'Okay, Emer. I'm doing okay.'

'I noticed you didn't bring much luggage.'

Hannah remained silent.

'Hannah?'

'I'm not sure if I'll be staying for too long.'

'Why ever not?'

Silence.

Hannah's stare remained fixed on the stars.

Emer pondered if Hannah might be unwell, if her nerves had come at her again – she'd a meltdown a couple of years back and had been on meds and received counselling, which helped. Found God, too. Of course. Which helped. Her. She'd never got over seeing the body in the furze. Sometimes the image is much less than blurred.

'You can tell me, Hannah. You do know that?'

Hannah looked at her and shook her head as she said, 'I don't think I can, you know?'

'Are you ill?'

'Let's talk about you instead, being shot at and shooting those two men.'

'Not tonight.'

'What does it feel like to have killed someone?' Hannah probed lightly.

'So you want to walk in my dark clouds, and yet you won't let me into yours – sounds like a bum deal to me.'

Hannah's chin rose a little in indignation.

Emer pressed, 'You sound like one of those women who wants to marry a man on death row... I haven't got round to really thinking about it – I think stuff like that hits me a bit down the line.'

Hannah said, 'Like with Mam and Dad's passing.'

'Like.'

'It was on Prime Time on TV,' Hannah said, 'and in all of the newspapers. They didn't mention you by name, just said an Irish officer was involved and a non-commissioned officer – everyone I heard speaking about it referred to you as being a man. They'll get a surprise, won't they, when the news eventually breaks. That the hot shot was a woman.'

'It'll break in the autumn when the court-martial begins – that's why I decided to spend a year here. By the time I eventually get home it'll all be old news,' Emer said with hope.

Opening a packet of crisps, she put a few flakes onto her palm.

'Have you got the Big C or something?' Emer asked, peering into the crisp packet – they put so bloody few chips into these nowadays. Especially those family packs.

'Always to the point... Of the mind, maybe,' came a quiet response. 'Or...'

'That's quite profound; of the mind,' Emer said.

'I don't know how you can eat those,' Hannah said. 'They keep slipping down into my gums and filling in the gaps between my teeth – I—'

'Let's stop the guff, Hannah, and spit it out.'

Hannah nodded several times and said, 'John...'

Emer saw in her sister's suddenly fraught expression a lit fuse leading to a bombshell revelation.

'John.'

'What about him, Hannah?'

What about my ex?

'I knew something about him and I didn't tell you – he begged me not to and he said he loved you and I believed him and...'

She's got to be fucking kidding me.

'Just say it, for fuck's sake,' Emer said.

'He cheated on you.'

Emer had never felt such an urge to clatter the head off her sister. She stood and went indoors, firmly sliding the patio door behind her; it shuddered slightly. In her bedroom, she locked the door, not so much to prevent Hannah from entering but as a small obstacle that might stall her from surrendering to the urge to say more than would be bad for either of them to hear.

She drew in several large breaths, held each and let go.

My God.

My... God. The bastard. I was right about him the whole time...

Can't sit with this, she thought, *without a cigarillo.* She couldn't remember where she kept her tiny emergency stash in the apartment and so went to her car.

Hannah, she'd noticed, hadn't stirred from the balcony, and did not dare look up to see her sister stride purposefully and noisily from the apartment. Hannah knew well enough to steer clear when her sister had worked up a head full of steam – but not so well to stop herself from saying the sort of thing that would light her fuse.

The car park was quiet and eerily silent. A streetlight blew just as Emer reached the car, spooking her a little. But she was angry enough to take on a horde of ghosts – even those cursed blue idols. She opened the glove compartment and lit a cigarillo. Decided to go for a drive, the tiredness forced from her. She reversed at speed and swung forward faster, rubber screeching against the asphalt.

Just gone 11:35. No idea as to where she might go – she simply wanted to expend juice – petrol and anger.

How many miles to Nazareth?

Drive. It doesn't matter.

Miles.

Her thoughts went in as many directions as destinations. Nazareth, Tiberias, Caesarea, the site of the Mount of Beatitudes, the location of the Miracle of the Loaves and Fishes.

Hannah should have upped and told her ages before about the cheating rat. It would have spared her a ton of anguish, thinking she was selfish in allowing her army career to be a deal-breaker. How could he look her in the eye after being with that other woman?

He'd made love to me after being with her.

For...

Rage rose to a splitting pain in her forehead. She lost track of time, took a wrong road, reversed and eventually pulled in at a spot overlooking Tiberias and the Sea of Galilee. She watched the sunrise streaking the water with soft gold, orange, and silver. She was low on petrol, but her temper and frustration were far from being spent. Then, she closed her eyes, levered the seat back, and half-dozed in the car. Panicked for moments as she surfaced fuzzy-headed from sleep, thinking about being late for work until realising that she had intended on bringing Hannah on a tour. Not happening.

She felt tired, spent and hungry too. Still in uniform, drab greens, her blue beret on the back seat.

Money?

Glove compartment – good – almost 50 shekels and some smaller coins. Enough to roll on down to Tiberias and breakfast, go to the bathroom. She needed to fill the car, too.

She checked her phone for messages and texts, before easing from the gravel patch. Nothing. She'd expected to receive at least one or a text from Hannah, a grovelling apology or a question asking where she had gotten to, if she was all right.

By early afternoon, she'd reached her apartment, creak-necked and stiff-legged from sleeping in the car. She carried a swollen bag of groceries in each hand – much like she had seen her mother often do; twine handles cutting into her palms, swaying a little from side to side, one bag heavier than the other. Do the scales ever sit evenly?

First she'd run the bath and soak herself, empty a bottle of wine, start on another and pig out on cartons of Chinese food she'd bought at the store.

Planned everything except how she was going to deal with Hannah.

With some luck, she thought, she might have taken herself elsewhere. Whatever she had to say to Hannah hadn't fully formed in thought, let alone in word.

No luck.

She was there, sitting cross-legged on the armchair, looking contrite. Emer met her eyes and drove them into finding a corner to peer into.

'I'm sorry, Emer.' The words limp, yet sincerely spoken.

Emer idly emptied the contents of the bags on to the counter, began to put them in either the fridge or the presses.

'Don't talk to me,' she said.

'I should have told you. But I didn't want to break up your marriage. You know I don't believe in divorce or—'

'Keep it to yourself.'

'We're not all like you.'

'What the hell does that mean? What am I like?'

'Hard.'

'Hard?'

Silence.

'So, I'm hard because I'm pissed off my husband went and fucked another woman and you, darling sister, who tells me everything that goes on in her life, kept her lips shut about some mega event got to do with mine.'

'I'm—'

'I don't want to hear your sorries. Who was she?'

Hannah's chin dived low.

'Do I know her?'

Hannah spluttered out the name.

'Her... Jesus... Her! She's pure ugly.'

Tears forming, Hannah folded her arms across her small breasts, kept her eyes from her sister's.

'The air has to be cleared on this, yeah, but not now, Hannah. There's another hugely pressing matter. It is probably not safe for you to be with me. In fact, it's not probable, it's a cast-iron fact. I shouldn't have let you come here.'

Hannah held her sister's stare and did not falter.

Emer told her all about it. Being followed, how people thought she had the idol, that people had already died because of it – how her boss thought she should carry a firearm at all times.

'I still want to stay, if you'll let me,' Hannah said.

'You wouldn't, not if I showed you a photo of the girl's body washed up against the rocks of Akko, Hannah. I keep thinking I'm going to find Casey's in that state, sometime in the future.'

'Still... I'd like to stay.'

'They might take you to blackmail me.'

'I'm staying.'

Emer thought to say that Hannah would never walk past a cross without wanting to be stuck to it but kept it to herself.

'I've got a bit of a medical procedure in two weeks,' Hannah admitted, 'a thyroid thing, yeah. It's not serious, but could be if I don't have it taken care of... That's the truth of it. This trip isn't a bucket list thingy.'

Emer crossed her lips with her forefinger for Hannah to speak no more about it. She hugged her sister.

Hannah said, 'So, am I staying?'

'You didn't pack much.'

'I'm buying myself a new wardrobe here – why not?'

'I'm going to shower and then we'll go for a drive. I'll bring you to Nazareth, Cana, a couple of other places, how's that?'

'Great, I'll make the coffee.'

'The other issue is parked until I get my head around everything else. Don't bring it up. But he's going to be in for a land when I tell him the grounds for divorce have been altered.'

Hannah nodded, averted her eyes. 'Ireland has a no-fault divorce policy.'

'Did you bring any good news, at all?'

CHAPTER 59

Ten days later, the sisters were well settled into a routine, with Hannah heading off on day trips to local places of interest, while Emer organised next month's operational activities with her staff.

When the office was empty she opened her grey canvas satchel and took out the .38 calibre revolver. Brand new, shiny brown holster. Read the manifest again, stamped in Hebrew and with the UNIFIL insignia, signed by Fredericksen and countersigned by an Israeli customs official. She would stop at the UN pistol range on the way to the border and fire off some practice rounds to get a feel for the trigger pressure and its range.

She recalled a shooting competition some years ago. A harmless administration course event held indoors, using air pistols. She'd topped the list by a single point and the second-placed man demanded a recount. The sergeant in charge, flustered by this unexpected intensity and lack of sportsmanship, reluctantly consented, and in front of the complainant went through the individual brown cardboard targets, each hit pen circled. He had indeed miscounted – she'd ended up winning by four points. The sergeant said she had a natural eye and she thought about that now – what was it to be a natural at doing something? Where did that skill come from? In her DNA? She wished she were natural at something else. But if that were the case, she would most likely be coffined already.

She poured coffee and ate a croissant for lunch, as she collated and proofread reports.

A knock. The handle already beginning to turn.

'Wait,' she said, putting the pistol and ammo and the weapon's cleaning material into her satchel.

When he entered, she said, 'Colonel Morris, this is a surprise. I haven't seen you in a while.'

'May I?' he said.

You knocked and entered without getting permission.

She presumed his, 'May I?' was implied sarcasm, and said nothing, leaving him to close the door.

'Busy?' he said, sitting on the chair behind her desk.

'Sir,' she said evenly, 'you're sitting at my desk.'

'Where do you suggest I sit?' he said.

'A pointed blade would do it for me.'

He smiled and stood, mimed a waiter showing a customer to her seat.

He sat on a chair at the side of her desk and angled it in such a way to afford him full eye contact.

'How can I help, sir?' she said.

'I'm not your enemy. I wanted you here for the year. You should know that. And Fredericksen; well, he rates you very highly. I do, too, by the way.'

'Only because you need someone to probe this historic abuse case and the associated missing children investigation.'

'I should have more information on that for you very soon.'

'So?'

'When this soldier arrives in Lebanon in October… it will begin – then the witnesses will announce their allegations in public. You can effect his arrest then.'

'If the evidence is solid.'

'It appears it is. He has no idea that this is going to happen. We need him to tell us where he buried the bodies. This could be explosive – when the news breaks, he could be a dead man walking, so we need to make sure he's not harmed.'

Their eyes locked for a second. As usual, she thought, *This fellow's not showing his entire hand.*

'How many bodies?'

'Three, but it could be more.'

'We can't even find Casey.'

'We will. Give it time. I mean, *you* will.'

'Why is this man returning – I mean – what's the lure? Is it to kill again? His surviving victims and their families will bay for his blood – he must know the risk he's taking, surely? He must have factored in that his victims could have already pointed the finger. And blindly ignores it.'

'All of that,' he said, 'is for you to find out. But he has no idea we are on to him. None. That, I can assure you of.'

She sighed, and said she'd love to hear more from him but she had to leave momentarily. 'On official business,' she said, smiling. He found it hard not to ask and it irked him that she would not divulge.

When he'd gone, she dwelt on the other piece of his news he'd delivered – there wouldn't be any Irish MPs coming out in the autumn. They were needed in Kosovo. She'd hoped for one to arrive. Realised, too, that she would see her present crew leave Lebanon before her – their service completes by end of the year in staggered rotations. This time next year a new team would be sitting and listening to her briefings. And she'd still have three months to serve before going home. After what Morris just told her, there might be even another demand for her to extend her tour of duty.

'It's a vocation, this job,' he said.

She would go and shoot some targets on the range.

Focus on her aim.

She wondered what Hannah was cooking tonight.

Steak?

She was not a good cook.

Hannah would be heading home too, in a few days.

What did Timo say he needed bringing down? she thought. *Oh, yeah, some clean T-shirts, a beer can or two.*

Hannah.

Probably wise for me to suggest that we should eat out at the Penguin.

CHAPTER 60

S he had found her way to Aunt Gretta by squeezing every mile out of the money she had been given. When she got near, she made a call to the kibbutz where she worked. There was a long silence before Gretta came to the phone. She'd listened and said to wait for her in town.

'I'll collect you there, Juliette.'

Her daughter's name, the baby who had died. Jenny was now Juliette Franz. Gretta's daughter, home from Europe. A daughter who had had several teeth shaken from her skull, a discoloured eye, who endured violent headaches and wildly disturbed dreams. Head shaved. T-shirt hanging off her sunken shoulders.

'Again,' Aunt Gretta said in her pale-yellow kitchen. Sunshine-filled.

And again, Jenny recited, without a blip, her new life history. She had Juliette's birth cert, her history imagined – born in Israel, moved to Ireland, and now back to live with her mother. People could check, but no one would bother. She would be a kibbutznik, would serve in the army – where she must pretend to know nothing of military training and so on. But that was ahead of her after she had healed. She would learn Hebrew. Learn her history. She must be as Juliette would have been, as close as humanly possible.

'Yes,' Jenny agreed, under her aunt's hard stare.

They moved outside and sat under the veranda, enjoying a drink of homemade lemonade, shaded from the scorching sun.

Gretta was first to see the car with the UN markings at the top of the U-shaped estate.

'Go inside… Hurry!'

Emer slowed and read the door numbers, searching for the one she'd been given by a man at the kibbutz office. There, where that young boy had left the veranda and gone indoors.

She ranged alongside a bed of orange flowers, alighted, and approached the woman, removing her blue beret.

'Mrs Franz,' Emer said, stopping at the bottom step of the veranda.

'Yes.'

'May I?'

'No. I can hear you from where you are. Why are you UN here? I said I didn't want to talk about the matter.'

'I'm trying my utmost to find your niece, Mrs Franz. Why won't you help?'

Gretta frowned and gestured for her to come forward. A beautiful blue bird flew up from the bushes. Emer caught the scent of honeysuckle and heard the buzzing of bees.

Seated, Emer asked, 'Have you heard anything from her?'

'No. What's more, I don't expect to – she stole my car and my money – she violated my trust, that's something I could never forgive. She's her mother's daughter, I say.'

'She's – do you think she's still alive?'

'How on earth would I know the answer to that? But if only the good die young…'

'Hmm.'

Nothing was said for moments.

'It was you who left the idol at the hotel.'

'I tried to help her – that's what makes what she did so difficult to accept.'

'How did you know where I was staying?' Emer asked, wanting to confirm.

'I called into the office in Jerusalem. Some man told me – he smiled at me the whole time I was there like there was nothing he wouldn't do for me.'

Pedney.

'A-ha. Okay. If Jenny gets in touch, will you let me know?'

'No.'

'No?'

'The Israeli police can notify you. They're the first ones I'll be calling if she puts her nose around here. You have my word on that.'

'Do you live alone?' Emer said.

'Mostly. I have people stay over from time to time.'

'Is that boy I saw leave, is he your son?'

'God, no. That's a youngster who helps with the garden for a few shekels.'

'This is a nice place,' Emer said. 'In fact, it's absolutely beautiful – tranquil.'

'Yes. When the Hezbollah aren't lobbing shells at us, it is.'

'Are you married?'

'Was. My husband died in the wars. I have a daughter who visits from time to time. I'm so glad she wasn't here when that other Jenny one came prowling along – Juliette's a crusader for every hopeless case.'

'Can I leave you my business card? Would you mind?'

'Sure. But like I said...'

No offer of tea. She's ultra distrustful. Maybe that's her default setting, Emer thought. *I suppose that's how people react when they've been badly let down. I wouldn't like to be Jenny if she arrives on this woman's doorstep looking for help.*

But she got the feeling that what Gretta said wasn't a neat stack of truths either.

CHAPTER 61

Hannah bought her two framed pictures as going-away presents – copies of the works of the Victorian artist David Roberts, who'd travelled across the Middle East in the 19th century. One of the Moorish keep at the UN camp, which stood behind the MP base, and the other of the isthmus at Tyre. Both of which Emer liked very much and would hang on the wall when she made up her mind where they should rest.

Hannah, tomorrow, would be home.

Twice, Hannah reported seeing a strange car drive slowly past her. But not in the last day or so.

Emer was after sending the lawyer handling her divorce an email appraising him of her sister's news, to see what he made of it, when her phone sounded.

Avi Cohen.

Has he got news of Casey?

No, but an invitation to dinner.

Take him up on it.

'I have information for you,' he said.

She had news for him, too. He said his son worked in Israel National Museum – if he did, it was under a different surname. She'd checked it out.

CHAPTER 62

Cohen was waiting for her in *Solomon's* U-shaped seaside restaurant in the old part of Akko, a halfway meeting point for them both, his suggestion.

The lights of Haifa across the bay shone like a series of fluorescent pearls, almost eerily, she thought. Auras of dying souls.

He was drinking lager. Maccabi label torn and wet at its edges. Moisture beads studded the dark brown bottle.

Henna-tinted hair. Avi.

God, she thought. Someone once told her that men who dyed their hair were trying to make up for a youth they had not properly lived, which somehow mysteriously passed them by. But Avi was not that old. Roughly the same age as her father was when he'd fallen terminally ill. Back then, she supposed, she'd probably considered him old.

The Israeli detective rose and lightly squeezed her hand and smiled broadly. Implants looked somewhat out of sync in an ageing face. He asked what she would like and she said a whiskey would be fine. 'I'm not driving – I've got an MP from my section picking me up whenever.'

'Meaning you're putting an oldish cop at ease – you're telling him that you won't be drink-driving or doing worse,' he said with an affecting smile.

'What could be worse?' she said, wishing she'd dressed up a little better for the occasion. He seemed to have gone the extra mile.

There was teasing in her tone. And she asked herself where that had come from, as it hadn't been intended.

'Ah, perhaps for you to make an old chap very happy.'

'Jesus, it's the last thing I would want to do, Avi.'

He smiled. 'So no confusion then, Miss Harte.'

She reached for the menu.

'You should try the tuna salad for starters,' he said.

'I'll have whatever you're having,' she decided, leaving the menu standing.

He chuckled. 'It's your choice of drink that matters most to you?'

'Of course. Do you mind if I smoke?'

He shrugged his bony shoulders. 'We're in the open air.'

She gazed at the calm sea water beneath the parapet beside their table and felt suffused with a good feeling, a sense of optimism. The setting provided balm for the apprehension she'd felt about the meeting. She'd pondered what his expectations might be, how he would react when he popped that question to her and heard her response. If indeed, he would hint.

It was the hair, the teeth. She couldn't... Oh, God, no. His age.

'How is your Timo Lahr these days?' Avi said.

'My Timo Lahr?'

'Not yet, so... In the future, maybe.'

'Are you married, Avi?'

'No. Divorced – about ten years now – we'd been married for close-on 30 years.'

'That's a long time.'

'Yes, we changed into people neither of us liked very much.'

'Are you on good terms with her?'

'Yes, these days we can be civil to each other. Occasionally it is an effort. And you...'

She told him about John.

He nodded like a sage and said, 'Better now than in 20 years' time.'

'I believe so,' she murmured.

She brought her whiskey to her lips, sipped from her glass as though it were liquid diamond she was savouring. Bushmills – she'd tasted it once before and hadn't been overly impressed, but now she found herself enjoying it very much. Every brand of whiskey deserves a second chance.

Once the waitress left with their order, he asked what was on her mind.

'What it is that you have to tell *me*, Avi, is on my mind.'

He wagged his forefinger and said, 'Ladies first.'

'I see. Well, you know how it is, Avi – something happens and there's a massive amount of paperwork to create. And when sifting through the reports, the statements, summaries and so on, missing information rises from the pages, like spectres – why wasn't this asked, why wasn't this verified, what did that person mean when he said that?'

He pulled a face – a face like well-tanned leather, lined and buffed by time and sunshine.

'I know of it only too well,' he said. 'And what are these spectres for you?'

'The photographs – have you got any of the actual shootout – and in particular, who stole the idol from Lahr's travel bag?'

He wore a blue, short-sleeved shirt and his forearms were thin and corded with veins, indicating a strength his frame did not otherwise suggest.

'No,' he said.

'Only it seems very convenient that those others were taken and none of the main event. No criticism intended, but as fellow police you understand I had to poise the question.'

'None taken,' he said firmly, lips tightening. Then, 'Anything else?'

'How is your son?'

'He is well.'

His tone made it difficult for her to ascertain his mood, and his expression was a blank map. His fawn-coloured eyes acquired an extra sheen as he said, 'I am happy that we have one of those idols in the Israel Museum – I do not believe in a god or gods or any nonsense rituals, but we have plenty of fanatics who do. These particular items are part of a sacrificial ritual – which means that innocents, children mostly, would be murdered for whatever sick purpose. So, yes, while I would love a second idol to be doubly sure that none of this sickness develops – I'm afraid, Emer, that we had nothing to do with it going missing.'

Sip your whiskey, she told herself.

'Does that answer your question?'

The food arrived; it smelt and tasted delicious. They ate in silence for minutes.

'Do you think the idol was quickly passed to Chief Joseph or the Polish MP at the ambush site, and they rushed northwards with it?' Cohen speculated.

'And they would have sold it to whom? They deny any knowledge of ever seeing the idol on that day.'

'Their eventual buyer is a Jewish rabbi... No name, Emer, your interest and jurisdiction ends with the UN personnel.'

'Do you have any idea who they passed it on to – if he was UN?'

'I would assume he is. But that is your loose end.'

She smiled. 'You'd have to kill me if you told me – or what, sleep with you?'

Crow's feet at the corner of one eye deepened, and his eyes sparkled as he said, 'No. I only sleep with women who want to sleep with me. Those who do, I'm very sad to relate, are becoming fewer and fewer as time wears on – but one lives in hope. Besides... There is no time.'

'No time?'

He glanced at his watch. 'A little for some more small talk, then we must part.'

What remained of her appetite went out on the back of a tiny wave that had broken against the parapet. She sighed and looked hard, far out to sea, suddenly cold to the pit of her stomach.

'Casey,' she said, 'one of our MPs might have killed her or he was an accomplice in the act at the very least. I'm thinking the worst. She could be alive – but I can't get a lock on any evidence, nothing. And our main suspects have been spirited away to their own countries to face trial on these and other matters. I keep hoping that Lahr had no part in it. He tells me he had none. It's hard to trust once trust has been broken, you know.'

'One of your own and an agent of mine had it in for her,' he said, slicing through a rib-eye steak. 'They were in it together.'

'I see,' she said, as she halved a crusty roll and spread butter on it, but merely to distract herself.

'I can reveal that she was seen in the company of this agent, Salah Ameer – a career criminal. He has previous convictions for arson, theft, and smuggling. People trafficking – he murdered the Colombian girl in Akko, who was wearing Casey's T-shirt because she gave him a smart answer and a kick to his shin.'

'Have you been in touch with him?'

'I didn't say he was a former agent.'

'Where was she seen with him?'

'In Akko, hereabouts.'

'So,' she said flatly.

'Is the food okay?'

'I'm no longer hungry.'

She understood he had drawn a line in the sand, for this evening; enough talking about the job. She was not quite done with her questioning, but there was nothing she could do about it – he was in full control.

'Salah Ameer,' she breathed, taking a chance there was still a small wind in Avi's sail.

'He is one of my informants,' he said, staring at the French fry at the end of his fork.

'A killer.'

'I can tell you this because I am due to retire in a few days. My new man is an odd one, let me tell you. So Salah, he is... sacked... and he is your quarry.'

'He's outside my jurisdiction, as you said.'

'Here is your dilemma, Emer – he's looking for you and Dabrowski's brother has put a price on your head for killing his brother and for stealing the idol.'

Blood drained from her face and the whiskey went straight to her head. Not news, but always terrifying to hear the fact said aloud.

'He will follow you to your grave – have no doubt. But he's busy for the next while, fighting a gang war on his own turf in Warsaw. If you're lucky, he'll lose.'

Silence, apart from the low wash of the sea, a gaggle of laughter from another table.

Emer aired in a strained voice, 'I feel like I've just being told that I've got a terminal illness.'

'In a way yes and no... Again, for what it is worth, I know exactly how you feel.'

'How did you deal with it?'

'I excised the cancer. Always. It works until someday it does not.' He got up and said, 'I have to go find someone to turn me out of bed happy. We won't see each other anytime soon. I will settle the bill on the way out.' Coughed before saying, 'Salah won't be there forever. Drugs wear off. There's a key in the door. He might tell you what he did with Casey's body. Dabrowski is another day's work if you're unlucky and he wins his war.'

'I—'

'I'll be in touch.'

'This Ameer is a present, for me?'

'Goodbye, Emer,' he said. He put his hand on her shoulder, and whispered in her ear, 'You dealt yourself into this. But you saved many lives by giving me the idol... so you did good, a lot of good. But I'm not going to kill for you. I only kill for my country. You need to finish this man, for your own future safety.'

Dealt myself in?

She disagreed and thought to say it was her superiors who'd involved her. Any good she did was inadvertently achieved. But she said nothing about this to the Israeli detective because she knew there was no point – and besides, Avi Cohen, she this very moment realised, was probably the most dangerous person she had ever met.

Now what?

She picked up the card – blank on one side, an address in blue biro on the other. Description, a lopsided gait, ginger hair, muscular...

'Think basement'... His last two erratically scrawled words.

Is this a set-up?

A scheme to save them from abducting her in some alleyway, where there might be witnesses? But she remembered a veteran soldier's advice about Lebanon – when a local advised you not to go down a certain street, heed the warning. They won't make a song and dance about imparting the advice – it might simply be a wagging of an index finger. Moments ago she'd received advice of a different kind. To go into the lair of the beast and slay the dragon in its bed. The name Avi gave her, half of it matched that breathed on the phone by Chief Joseph, that she'd heard on Sven's recording.

The revolver, nursed in its holster in her shoulder bag, lay at her feet. Like some rare cure she should only use to save her life – even though the side-effects might prove as toxic.

Did she really want to kill another human being?

Had she got it in her to squeeze the trigger? Again.

But that been done on instinct in a kill-or-be-killed situation.

This would be different; this would require shooting someone in cold blood.

And his death, it seemed, would be only part of the cure. Buying time.

She would do it, for herself, for her foolish sister, for anyone else Salah might kill or try to kill in the future. Most of all, she would do it for the young woman whose body was washed up on the rocks, deaf to the quiet song of the sea...

CHAPTER 63

Almost 9 o'clock. Her stomach played three strands of anxiety at once, a ziggurat of sorts, as she moved along the tight flagged lanes of the ancient city. Shuttered shops steel-lipped against the salt air and the night. Shutters with locks like gold teeth with silvery upside-down 'U's bolstered against the world. Streetlights burned against the night, a ship's klaxon sounded distant, somehow vaguely, apologetically blowing across the sea. Her mind raced. Her stomach quivered and her knees felt weak. Perspiration sequined her forehead, dampened her hair. A slick of moisture crawled icily along her spine.

Here?

Burj Hammoud Street, a narrow cul-de-sac. So tight a rat would have to back out of it, she thought.

Dark.

A café at one corner of the alley shuttered. At the other a stout red door flanked by windows grilled with bars. Not another soul.

She slipped into the alley, revolver by her side, hammer poised, safety off, the first pad of her forefinger on the trigger – she knew its squeeze, how much pressure she should apply. Wished for a Magnum with a velocity to kick him back several feet, take his head clean off his shoulders.

Inhaled. Exhaled.

A stirring to her right, at a wheely bin. A cat meowed loudly, jumped on top of a dead-end wall partly adorned with shards of broken glass cemented in place. A door to her left, ajar. Nudged open with the tip of her revolver.

Small hall, stairs scaling it at a steep gradient, the landing unseen, shaded in blackness. A musty and mildew odour pushed into her nostrils, made her gag.

Another door to her right she guessed would open to the café. Pressed down on the handle, took in a breath and pushed, moving quickly yet as stealthily as the cat had done moments before. She dropped to her knee, shoulder bag slapping against her thigh.

Silence.

The room was dimly illuminated by the artificial glow from a vending machine.

She'd an awareness of tables and chairs, smelt the presence of congealed food and another of a cleanser. Turned on her pen torch as she stood, keeping it atop the gun's muzzle.

Its light revealed islands of tables with chairs seated on them, behind her a counter, and behind it shelves holding containers of foodstuff.

There.

A curtain of multi-coloured plastic strips. She moved toward it, and when she'd passed through, the strips slapped against her shoulder blades. The bar of weakish light showed stairwells that climbed and descended.

Basement?

Bare wood, thick slats, margins filmed with dust. The door. The key. She turned it and shouldered the door gently. Reached around in search of a light-switch, keeping her bar of light on the stairwell. Didn't find it. Boards creaked under her weight, the light piercing the gloominess as she went step by careful step to the last one, where she drew up short to survey the area. Cluttered with cardboard boxes, cleaning supplies, pallets of bottled water and soft drinks.

She had expected a bedroom.

Why had she thought that?

There was a cot covered with a blanket against a wall, nearby a sturdy chair with a thick red rope hanging loosely around its legs. Lengths of rope and plastic ties.

He's freed himself. Has he fled the building? Is he here? Has Avi set me up?

Advanced to ground level.

Heard a movement and as she half-turned, a huge weight powered into her frame, sending her crashing into empty cardboard boxes and fruit crates. Her trigger finger involuntarily squeezed as the revolver spilt from her grasp. Ricocheted several times... *Ping, ping, ping.*

He was strong. Brute. Emer squirmed as he tried to snare her wrists to the ground. She drove the heel of her hand toward the centre of his face. Bone shattered – the sound of a twig being snapped. He roared. Then a muffled cry, fuelled with pain and utter rage.

Her rib. Emer thought she'd been run through with a sword. Put her hand there, wet.

Shit...

He pushed against boxes, sending some flying.

Heard the sticking of the knife in cans and bottles.

She crouched, gritting her teeth.

The revolver?

Her bag? Pepper spray.

If his nose was pumping, it might affect his vision.

Emer, it's completely fucking dark! she snapped at herself. They both might as well be blindfolded.

Pitch black, but he would guard the stairwell.

Think... Think.

One hand on her wound to staunch the flow of blood, the other groping blindly ahead came into contact with rope – the chair. She drew in the rope, creating a dragging noise from the movement of

243

the chair.

'Avi sent you, didn't he?' he said, words issued through a bloodied mouth.

She remained silent.

'To insult me, to have a woman kill me.'

Flow from the water bottles and soft drinks he had pierced reached her feet.

She crawled slowly on her side, behind a row of pallets, and stopped. Listened. She hoped he had not climbed the steps, to turn on a light. He would know where the switch was. Inch by inch, in agony, she eased her way toward the stairs – where she thought they were – hoping she wouldn't end up going about in circles. If he turned on the light he would see her in an instant. He might still be groggy from the drugs and the clip to his nose – so she needed to work those to her advantage before their effects wore off.

Please, God, don't let there be anything blocking me from getting in under the stairs.

So close, she could hear him breathing – rasping, snorting – the sound of a cat with a blocked nose.

Her fingers touched wood. Ran them a distance at an angle, upwards. Yes. Steps.

Yes.

She slipped under the stairs, behind him. Fed the rope out on to the second step, in a wide loop. Strengthened her grip on both ends.

'There's no way out,' he said.

He spat a goblet of phlegm into the blackness.

She heard a hesitant creak. Another.

A click of a switch. Light...

'When I get you – I'm going to make you suffer.'

He stood with both feet on the stairs. The blood from his nose dropped in small beats on the timber, like the sound of raindrops. She heard the creaking stair and pulled hard on the rope. Leaned back as though she were using oars, so hard she almost fainted from the pain in her side, but he was down, falling head-first in a crashing cascade of flesh and bone.

Silence.

Apart from the emptying of a burst soft drink can, losing its fizziness, silence.

Sliding from under the stairs, she watched him for any sign of movement. A shard of glass protruded just below his right eyeball. His head turned at an unnatural angle. She swept her eyes along the wet floor and saw the revolver and her bag. Hurried to retrieve both, shouldered her bag, aimed the revolver at him. Pointlessly.

Checked her wound. Not deep. But it hurt like hell.

She turned him over, patted down his shirt, studied the bloodied broken nose, the blood spatters on his short fringe and ginger hair. Glassy green eyes. No notes in his shirt pockets. She removed his Samsung mobile phone, searched for the shell and slug from her revolver, finding only the casing; the slug could have come to rest anywhere.

'Why bother searching for it?' she whispered, her wound biting.

I can't eradicate all of the evidence that places me here: my blood, for starters. The fabric of my clothing would have mixed with Salah's... Every contact leaves a trace.

She left as she had come, through the winding alleyways. At the seafront, she rang for her MP escort to collect her nearby. With some tissues from her bag, she cleaned up as best she could. Did up the buttons on her jacket to cover the wound. While she waited she considered throwing Salah's phone into the sea. It was what she wanted to do when she thought of him holding his mouth and ear to it, his sweat on the receiver. But she didn't because she couldn't – who knew what information it might contain? Its battery was flat, so she couldn't check. But Avi would have taken it... if he thought it worthwhile.

She did not speak on the drive back. Once she reached the apartment, Hannah, shaking with a kind of nervous energy, dressed her wounds. Several times she urged Emer to go to the hospital in Haifa, but her sister stood firm. No.

Hannah gave her a double dose of painkillers and sat with Emer on the balcony, not saying a word, watching her as she looked up silently at the stars.

Casey… Was that where she'd been imprisoned?

Bound by those ropes in that same chair?

'I'll sleep here,' she said, and Hannah left her alone with her glass of neat whiskey, her cigarillos, a warm blanket, and a gnawing pain. Sapped of energy, emotionally and physically – two dead men to her name – Emer took three sleeping pills and waited for their temporary relief to drift through.

CHAPTER 64

For days she waited for someone, something to bring news of the killing, but no one had; Salah's death hadn't registered even in the Israeli media, at least not in *The Jerusalem Post* or on Israeli TV. Cohen's doing?

Days later, Esther drove her back from the UN hospital. She had her dressing changed on the quiet by a nurse who would keep it off the books. Afterwards she looked in on Timo, who was sleeping.

The prefix was European, Finnish international prefix. It was Kirsten, the call Emer had expected for weeks.

'Esther, turn around and bring me back to the hospital,' she said.

She was already turning, sensing what the call had meant.

Lahr was due for discharge several times from hospital but each time the infection to his wound returned. His immune system was low, his mood lower.

She waited outside the hospital, paced up and down a row of palm trees, preparing herself, only entering the hospital when she knew she was in some way ready.

After drawing the chair to the side of his armchair, he said, 'I was watching you walking up and down outside. Did you see the giant lizard they talk about so much?'

She rubbed his upper arm.

'No,' she said.

'Emer. You don't have to tell me.'

She swallowed hard.

'You know, Timo. You know she's gone.'

247

'I saw it in your face.'

She watched as his tears ran silently and unchecked, his hand in hers. She did not utter a single word, offered no platitudes, she simply sat there, and stayed.

CHAPTER 65

Weeks later, the days grinding toward October, she had fully recovered from her injury. No more twinges – a scar a reminder, a permanent charm. *I collect them.*

Current investigations included a break-in, a suicide, an attempted suicide, and a fatal traffic accident; these she'd delegated to her staff.

Hannah had breezed out of her life and back to Ireland. Although a vein of anxiety about her upcoming operation ran through her like a tunnel in the old city of Jerusalem, she had left happy, weighed down with bric-a-brac, religious relics, and bottles of holy water from a tap in Bethlehem.

Emer kept the apartment in Nahariya. Why not? At least for the time being.

Fredericksen seemed to be switching off now that he had a handle on things. He liked to play golf, and spent much time in Beirut, preferring Lebanon to Israel, or Palestine as he sometimes called it. He had a definite date for his rotation to Norway.

Emer dreaded the thoughts of going home in October, knowing for the two weeks she'd be there – perhaps even one week longer – she'd be sitting in the same room as the man who tried to murder her. She hoped his missing arm haunted him forever and a day, acquire an itch he would never be able to scratch. Then... The divorce...

Once the court-martial was finished she would return and see if the cold case Morris had discussed would re-activate as he'd predicted. She had yet to turn her thoughts fully toward the investigation. It was going to be messy; she had no doubt.

Lahr had returned to Finland and rang her now and then to say he missed her. She admitted to a fondness for him, too. She'd no idea where the relationship was going but expected to get a handle on it during a five-day break in Helsinki. Her flight left in forty-eight hours. Lahr was going to be suffering in a lot of ways for a long time. He'd have a problem if he weren't hurting, she'd told him. It proved he was normal. His old laugh returned for a moment. Maybe he was beginning to get over the line?

It was a glorious morning as she made her way from the International Dining Complex, passing the helipad, entering the MP base. She might stay here tonight – she had her billet for whenever she was on call as Duty Officer. The day after tomorrow she would be in Finland. Fredericksen chuckled there was no chance of him cancelling her leave – he was no longer so brave.

A routine day, now.

The office was empty. She looked at the five desks, the filing cabinets, the pair of safes tucked in between them like two de-horned dwarf rhinos.

Emer drew the keys for the safes from her desk drawer and drummed up the codes in her head as she went to them. Twisted the dial on the nearest safe, applied the key. Shelves with bagged and tagged items of evidence, stacked willy-nilly, not an inch of space: drugs, knives, a blood-stained wallet, a suicide note, money, a machete, jewellery. She looked at each piece, noting the date, and then restocked the shelves, thinking to ask Fredericksen to requisition a larger safe. The other safe was just as crammed with evidence. Once more, she unpacked shelves, dwelling on the coins and small antiquities recovered from the Casey investigation. Looking at the Greek coins she found herself wondering about the people who hand-held these centuries ago, what they were like. It was, she supposed, the stirring of a new interest for her.

The idol.

She pictured it as she closed up both safes, twisted the dials, turned the locks. It was with someone... Who had Chief Joseph and Benny Rafal given it to? Had they crossed the border at Metula and managed to sell it on? Her gut told her no. Those guys were merely mules.

Seated behind her desk, she watched through the window the dog handler bringing her labrador for a walk. A sweet wrapper danced its way the length of the volleyball court.

'You're in dreamland,' a voice interrupted.

Morris.

'Sir,' she said, standing to face him.

He sat down. 'About October.'

'About October?'

He updated her – there hadn't been much change. Boland was still not talking, didn't want to plea for a deal in exchange for information.

She hid her displeasure at hearing a deal had been *offered* to him. If Boland had accepted it... God... She pictured herself attempting to shove her beret down Morris's throat.

'O'Rourke,' he said, scratching at the corner of his eyebrow, 'has been offered a deal in exchange... He handed up one of the missing idols.'

She let that last piece of information sink in – the tour party organiser, the person the girls had ripped off, believing that he was too weak-willed, too cowardly to do anything about it.

'Jesus,' she said. 'How did he get it home? I searched his bags, his billet... The works.'

'Simple. He sent it home as parcel post through the French Post Office.'

She walked past that post office almost every other day. 'Right under our noses.'

'Under our noses, yes – we've handed it over to the Iraqi

authorities,' he said. 'They were absolutely delighted to receive it.'

'Did O'Rourke tell you how he came to have it in his possession?'

'Well, let's just say that he was in the vicinity of the shooting.'

'So he drove the Jeep away? The one found in the scrapyard?'

'It would appear so. One idol down, one to find,' he said, eyeing her carefully.

'Eh... One more, yes.'

'I understand,' he said, 'that you're less than agreeable to deals being put in place. In O'Rourke's case, let's just say our government is planning on resurrecting its beef trade with the Iraqis. It was a hugely lucrative trade before the Iran-Iraq broke out.'

'There's always a bigger picture,' she said quietly.

He stood and looked at his watch. 'I've got a meeting to make – I'll be in touch to discuss this historical case... It's full of awfulness and shame.'

When he was gone, she sat, numbed. The dog handler and the black labrador had moved on, the sweet wrapper had moved on.

An hour later, her phone sounded. She let out a sigh – she was making good headway on her report and resented the interruption; it was difficult to pick up properly where she'd left off.

'Emer.'

Avi Cohen.

'I hadn't expected to hear from you again,' she said, her mouth suddenly falling dry.

'Always expect the unexpected.'

'You can sing that one.'

'I'm so glad you are well. I must admit to having been a little light on the drugs with Salah.'

'Deliberately.'

'I gave you a fighting chance though, you must admit.'

'Avi, why?'

'Why give you a fighting chance? I like you, and you brought me the idol. Karma is important. I'm at that age where I probably need to invest in creating good karma. And I think you're a little like me.'

'I don't think so.'

'Tell me, Emer – have you lost many sleepless nights thinking about the men you killed?'

'A couple. They wouldn't be dead if they hadn't tried to kill me. I keep telling myself that and I find it helps.'

'Good. When you're tasked to take someone out for the security of your country, without a shred of proof that the target intends to commit a terrorist attack – what justification will you use afterwards?'

'That's not going to happen.'

'I said the same.'

Pause.

'I've sent you a video recording, Emer. You'll understand when you see it. I'll be in contact with you again, sometime.'

He hung up.

Her phone pinged as the file downloaded. She played the clip immediately. Blackness filtering to a ceiling light in a basement and under it lay Salah. She was standing over him. Her revolver out, her face as clearly visible as a full moon unblemished by cloud.

'Bastard,' she whispered.

Emer stared at her stilled image and then deleted the recording. The taste of the discussion lay sour on her tongue. She powered off her laptop, craving now the sharp flow of whiskey down her throat. Yes. He'd be in touch again – he had left her in no doubt.

ABOUT THE AUTHOR

Lake Isle of Innisfree, photo by Valerie Malone

Martin (Murt) Malone is a distinguished Irish author with extensive field service in Lebanon and Iraq as part of UNIFIL and UNIIMOG. He holds a Master's Degree in the Philosophy of Creative Writing from Trinity College Dublin and has taught English to war and economic refugees from the Middle East and Europe. Currently lives in Kilmead, Athy, County Kildare, with his wife Valerie.

In the words of one of his characters:

"There are people who see no good in anyone, though there's a vestige of good in everyone. Those blind to this are the most dangerous of human beings—for not seeing this vestige in others, and worse, not in themselves."

Printed in Great Britain
by Amazon